PERFECT

BECKY BELL

Perfect Slave Abroad published by
Chimera Books Ltd
PO Box 152
Waterlooville
Hants
PO8 9FS

Printed and bound in Great Britain by
CPI Cox & Wyman, Reading.

ISBN 978-1-901388-47-3

New Authors Welcome

This novel is fiction – in real life practice safe sex

This book is sold subject to the condition that it shall not, by way of trade or otherwise, be lent, resold, hired out or otherwise circulated without the publisher's prior written consent in any form of binding or cover other than that in which it is published, and without a similar condition being imposed on the subsequent purchaser.

The characters and situations in this book are entirely imaginary and bear no relation to any real person or actual happening.

Copyright © Becky Bell
First printed in 1999. Re-printed in 2011

The right of Becky Bell to be identified as author of this book has been asserted in accordance with section 77 and 78 of the Copyrights Designs and Patents Act 1988.

PERFECT SLAVE ABROAD

Becky Bell

Chimera *(kī-mîr'ə, kĭ-)* a creation of the imagination, a wild fantasy

Marie-Claire rose gracefully. She always wore the same expensive perfume, a musky aroma that was wafted on the air by the movement of her peignoir. She moved behind Andrea and cupped the splendid curves of her buttocks, caressing them softly. Andrea gasped. Yesterday she had been caned twice, morning and evening. As far as she was concerned the cane was a hundred times worse than any whip and it left far worse marks; weals that actually puckered her skin. As Marie-Claire's hand deliberately stroked against them they tingled. The sensation was not altogether unpleasant.

Chapter 1

The basque felt cold against her skin. It made her shiver. She felt the laces being drawn tight, cinching her waist until it was narrowed and pinched, the bones of the corset biting into her and making her breathless. It was not a modern garment, made from silky pliant materials, but old-fashioned, its black and red satin lined with cambric and as stiff as a board. It was also much longer than modern versions and though it was strapless, its unyielding grip extended right down over her hips.

With one final effort the girl used every last ounce of her strength to pull the laces even tighter, making Andrea gasp as the basque closed around her. Apparently satisfied it could be cinched no tighter, the girl tied the laces off.

The bra of the basque was low cut and edged with frills of lace and Andrea's firm breasts swelled out of it, the upper hemisphere of the dark band of areola just visible. She had been made to wear this particular garment before and knew that the tightness of the laces was not its only torment. A metal clip had been sewn into the middle of each bra cup, the cold metal digging into her soft flesh. The girl reached into the bra, pushing Andrea's breast aside, then opened the clip and centred it on Andrea's nipple, letting its wickedly serrated jaws close around the poor bud.

Andrea gasped again. However accustomed she had become to the way her nipples and breasts had been tortured over the past weeks, she was sure she'd never become inured to the pain, nor to the extraordinary wave of pleasure - vivid pleasure - that inevitably followed. The second clip produced an identical response.

Sophia smoothed the bra cups back into place. She was a redhead, her hair wavy and thick. She was dressed in a tight white rubber catsuit that fitted her like a second skin, and white patent leather ankle boots with a spiky high heel. The catsuit had a circular cut-out around her navel that displayed her flat abdomen and the undersides of her small but firm breasts.

'Now the stockings,' she said.

Andrea picked up the stockings Sophia had left on the seat of a plain wooden chair, then sat on it to put them on. The material was black and silky, and as she pulled the stockings up her long slender legs it was as if she were coating them with glossy wet paint. Above the jet-black welt, the flesh of her thigh, by contrast, appeared creamy and soft. She clipped the stockings into the ruched satin suspenders of the basque.

'Stand,' Sophia said with her usual imperious tone. She indicated a pair of red high heels that she had placed on the floor. Andrea climbed into them. Even after two weeks of daily wear she hadn't got used to the height of the heels she had been required to wear, and found herself swaying to try and keep her balance.

Steadying herself she put her wrists together behind her back by rote, knowing Sophia would want to bind them there. She had never been allowed to leave what she'd come to think of as her cell without being in some form of bondage.

Sophia picked up a pair of leather padded cuffs and buckled them tightly around Andrea's wrists. She then took a length of white nylon rope and wound it around Andrea's upper arms, pulling it so tight her elbows were almost touching, the corded rope cutting deeply into her flesh.

'Comfortable?' Sophia asked. She enjoyed her work. She had never lost an opportunity to taunt, tease and torment Andrea above and beyond her instructions. She had pinched, prodded and probed Andrea's body on every possible occasion, taking pleasure from her discomfort, exactly as she was doing now, pulling Andrea around to face her and hugging her tightly. This was not a gesture of affection. She knew the clips built into the basque would be pressed back by her own bosom to cause a sharp twinge of pain. She smiled.

'Kiss me,' she purred.

But before Andrea could obey the redhead caught hold of her lower lip and nipped it between her teeth. She moved one hand up behind Andrea's back and held her neck so she could not pull away as she plunged her tongue into her mouth. However much Andrea detested the idea of kissing her tormentor she knew better than to refuse. Sophia needed only the slightest excuse to report her to Marie-Claire, so she closed her eyes and returned the kiss passionately, sucking on the tongue and letting it dance against her own. In the darkness she imagined she was kissing Charles Hawksworth, her master. But the illusion was difficult to sustain. Before she had met Charles, before she had been drawn into the extraordinary web of submission and domination in which he was involved, she'd never had sex with another woman and it was still a new enough experience for her to be overwhelmed by it. The image of Charles Hawksworth faded as she felt Sophia's voluptuous body moulding to her.

Without breaking the heady kiss the redhead pushed her leg up between Andrea's thighs, rubbing it against the nylon stockings, then moving it higher, until the white rubber was hard against Andrea's labia. She felt Sophia flex the muscles of her thigh, and knew the rubber would be smeared with the juices that were already leaking from her sex.

'Pity we don't have more time,' Sophia said huskily, stepping away. 'But madam is waiting.'

She had spent a long time on Andrea's make-up, but the kiss had smudged the dark red lipstick she'd applied so meticulously. Carefully she redrew it with a brush, then took Andrea by the arm and led her out.

The 'cells' were in fact small windowless rooms constructed of concrete breeze-block in part of a vast cellar in the eighteenth century chateau from which Marie-Claire Vuittenez ran her curious establishment. As far as Andrea had been able to discover Marie-Claire was hired by the various masters in what she had heard called *The System*, to train the women they brought to her to become their slaves. The training was not designed to ensure absolute obedience - which was taken for granted as a requisite of all her charges - but to enable them to perform the sexual tasks that would be required of them more adroitly. In her youth Marie-Claire had been a highly paid prostitute at one of the most famous of all Parisian brothels, or so she had told Andrea one night. She had married one of her clients, a count, who had been only too happy to allow his chateau to be used as a basis for her activities, bearing in mind the large number of nubile and beautiful young women who would pass through his new wife's hands would all be taught to practice their techniques on him.

There were four cells in all; a corner section of the brick vaulted cellar sealed off from the rest of the space. A staircase had been installed that led directly to a large addition to the original sixteenth century chateau which was specifically used for training.

At the top of the stairs there was a long corridor with a polished wooden floor. The two women's spiked heels clacked on the wood. Sophia took her right down to the far end and opened a door on the right.

'In,' she said, pushing Andrea forward with unnecessary force.

The room beyond was decorated to resemble a *fin-de-siècle* boudoir, no doubt a replica of the sort of rooms Marie-Claire Vuittenez had inhabited in her youth. It had a large elaborately carved four-poster bed, an equally ornate sofa upholstered in rich damask red, and a huge gilt mirror that took up most of one wall. Marie-Claire herself was sitting in a low Louis XV gilt-wood marquise armchair with her feet up on a matching footstool. There was a small table beside her, standing upon which was a silver wine cooler containing a bottle of champagne bathed in ice. She held a tall crystal champagne flute in heavily jewelled fingers.

'Good evening, my dear,' she said.

'Good evening, madam,' Andrea responded at once. She caught a glimpse of herself in the big mirror. Her long blonde hair had been brushed out over her bare shoulders, the incredibly tight corset forcing her figure into an hourglass shape, the voluptuous camber of her breasts spilling out at the top matched by the flaring curves of her hips. The high heels made her long legs seem even longer, their contours firmed by the muscles it was necessary to flex to keep her legs in that position.

'Tell Simone we're ready, would you, Sophia?'

'Certainly madam,' Sophia said, turning on her

heels and closing the door behind her.

'Come closer, child,' Marie-Claire said, beckoning elegantly with her free hand.

Andrea moved closer. She felt her pulse beginning to pound. Being in Marie-Claire's presence inspired a peculiar set of emotions. In the time she had been in training the woman had caused her great pain; but it was always a pain that had been swiftly followed by almost unbelievable sexual pleasure. She had come to associate the one with the other. So while Andrea feared her mistress she could not rid herself of an overwhelming sexual anticipation too.

Marie-Claire had the lightest blonde hair she had ever seen, so fair it seemed to radiate light. She was fairly short and slender, and always wore very heavy make-up. Though Andrea had no idea how old she was, she sensed her shapely body belied her age. This evening she was wearing a lush black chiffon peignoir edged with red lace, under which Andrea could see a black satin teddy.

'I have news for you,' she said, moving her hand to stroke Andrea's leg just above the knee. 'I have reported to your master that your training is almost complete. He has made arrangements for you to be sent back to London.'

Andrea felt her heart leap. The thought of seeing Charles again gave her an instant jolt of arousal. 'Thank you, madam,' she said.

Marie-Claire rose gracefully. She always wore the same expensive perfume, a musky aroma that was wafted on the air by the movement of her peignoir. She moved behind Andrea and cupped the splendid curves of her buttocks, caressing them softly. Andrea gasped. Yesterday she had been caned twice, morning and evening. As far as she was concerned the cane was a hundred times worse than any whip and it left far worse marks; weals that actually puckered her skin. As Marie-Claire's hand deliberately stroked against them they tingled. The sensation was not altogether unpleasant.

'So sensitive,' Marie-Claire whispered. She moved her hands up the front of the basque. 'I used to wear a corset just like this,' she said, her hands moulding into Andrea's waist. 'Without the clips, of course.' Her hands reached Andrea's breasts and squeezed them back against her chest so her nipples and the clips that bit into them were crushed. 'They were my idea. Do they hurt?'

'Yes, madam.'

'But that is not all they do, is it, my sweet?'

'No madam.'

'Tell me.'

'They make me...' It was hard to describe. The serrated jaws cut deeply into the tender flesh. After a while the nerves became numb but if they were provoked again, as Marie-Claire was doing now, they seemed to react with double the pain. It was not only pain, however. It was not as simple as that. There was a mechanism in Andrea's body that could translate pain into something quite different; a pleasure that was entirely rooted in her sexual being, as deep and profound as anything she had felt before. It was a mechanism that had been well exercised during her time at the chateau.

'Hot?' Marie-Claire suggested.

'Yes, madam.' It was exactly the right word. The pain and the pleasure it created heated her blood. She felt her vagina clench, the sticky sap of her body running down the tight silky tube.

'That is because you are a masochist. I, on the other

hand, derive sexual pleasure from delivering pain, as I'm sure you have come to realise.' She smiled. She had thin lips that gave her smile a menacing quality. 'We have both been fortunate to find out from which side of the cup we like to drink.' She moved around in front of Andrea again, examining her body critically. 'I have spent an inordinate amount of time torturing and tormenting both men and women.' A little smile flickered over her lips.

There was a gentle knock on the door.

'*Entrée.*'

The door opened and a man walked in. He was naked apart from a bizarre pair of black leather briefs. The front of the briefs was split and a series of eyelets had been inserted on either side of the opening. His genitals had been forced through the opening, which was then laced up tightly with leather thongs threaded through the eyelets. His cock stuck out from this arrangement, erect and glistening as if it had been oiled, every vein standing out prominently. The man's hands were held behind his back in metal handcuffs and a chain ran down from them to another set of metal cuffs that manacled his ankles together, making it impossible for him to take more than shuffling steps.

Andrea had come a long way in the short period since she'd first met Charles Darrington Hawksworth. There was a time when the sight of a man bound and so obscenely displayed would have shocked her to the core. Now it was simply commonplace. The man was a complete stranger but in a few moments, she knew, she would be asked to perform the most intimate sexual acts with him and would do so willingly. Though everything she did in the chateau was at the command of Marie-Claire, in reality she was only acting as an agent for Charles, her master. Everything Andrea did she did for him. She was his slave.

It had been hard to come to terms with that at first because she'd been so totally unaware of her needs. For some reason she did not properly understand Charles Hawksworth had known her better than she'd known herself. He had reached deep into her psyche and revealed emotions and desires that affected her in a way nothing else ever had. She discovered what she was capable of, and had come to realise that submission and bondage and absolute obedience gave her a satisfaction so deep-rooted and profound that she found it hard to believe she could have lived so long without it. She had come to see that what Charles offered her, the chance to be his slave, was an opportunity she could not turn her back on.

But being his slave, devoted and obedient to him, was very different from acknowledging that her obedience must include serving whomever he saw fit to give her to. The hardest thing had been to accept that not only was it necessary for her to obey his friends and his guests as obediently as she would obey Charles himself, but that he was prepared to send her away from him altogether. In fact, when he had taken her to the chateau she nearly refused to let him leave her there. Nearly, but not quite. She realised that if she were truly his slave she must obey without question *whatever* he ordered her to do however much she might dislike it. Her wishes were no longer important.

That had been a turning point, she knew. Agreeing to stay at the chateau meant she would be away from him for the first time. What's more, at the end of her period of training she would have to agree to be assigned to a new master for a period of six months before being returned to Charles. If she refused to agree to these conditions she would be sent home at once and would never have been allowed to see Charles again, under any circumstances. It was that prospect, the idea that she would not only be cut off from her master, but from the complex and arcane world that surrounded him, that had finally convinced her to stay. It was an irrevocable step as far as she was concerned, but despite the punishments and the pain she had received at Marie-Claire's hands over the last two months, she did not regret it. She had faced the truth. She was a slave. She needed to be a slave and she wanted to be a slave. It was as simple as that. Everything she did, everything she was asked to do, she did because she could see Charles Darrington Hawksworth's deep steel-blue eyes watching her.

'Bring him over here, Simone,' Marie-Claire said.

A tall olive-skinned woman with dark brown eyes had walked into the room behind the man. She had dark brown hair that looked as if it had been cropped and was only just starting to grow back, and was wearing a pair of skin-tight hot pants, made from a material that looked like liquid silver, and a pair of black ankle strap high heels. A bra-shaped network of thin black leather straps, which pinched the firm round flesh slightly but did not cover it, surrounded her breasts.

Simone took hold of the large ring in the front of a thick collar that was buckled around the man's neck, and pulled him forward, the chain around his ankles rattling. As he shuffled past her, Andrea saw the leather briefs had another rather unusual feature. At the back, instead of covering his buttocks, the gusset divided into three thin strips between his legs, one following the cleft of his arse while the other two wrapped around the outside of each buttock before rejoining the waistband, leaving his bottom completely exposed. The white and muscular flesh was marked, each buttock bearing a scarlet cross of weals, as neat as if they had been drawn on with a red pencil.

'Kneel,' Marie Claire said.

The man thumped to his knees in front of her immediately.

'I see Simone has been entertaining you.' Marie-Claire raised her left foot. She was wearing open-toed red satin high-heeled slippers. She touched her toes against his rampant cock.

'Yes, madam,' he said. He did not look up at her, his eyes firmly rooted to the floor.

'What is this on your cock, Patrick? This wetness?'

'Her juices, madam.'

'Really? Andrea, get down here. Clean this mess up.'

Andrea knew better than to hesitate. Orders had to be obeyed immediately. Her training had instilled that into her.

With her arms bound so tightly behind her back it was difficult to get to her knees softly and, like the man, she slumped to the floor. Quickly she bent right forward until her face was resting against his knees. Pushing herself up his legs she reached his cock and began to lick it. She tasted the unmistakable sweetness of a female's spending as she lapped at his hard shaft. It was only when she got this close to him that she saw the strange arrangement that surrounded the top of his cock. A circle of extremely thin black rubber tubing looped around underneath the ridge at the bottom of his glans. Stretched across the middle of this and fitting into the natural cleft in his glans and over the opening of his urethra was another strip of the same material. It was so tight it cut into the glans, deeply dividing into two hemispheres and, as she licked right up over it, she could see that this upper tubing was designed to hold another, much thicker piece of rubber tubing in the hole of the urethra itself.

'My own design,' Marie-Claire said, as if reading Andrea's mind. 'You would be astonished at how effective it is at delaying orgasm. Isn't that so, Patrick?'

'Oh yes, madam,' he croaked.

'All the men hate it. Which is an added bonus. Of course, it cannot prevent ejaculation totally, but it certainly spoils their fun.' She smiled cruelly. 'Have you licked him clean?'

'I think so, madam,' Andrea said. Simone's juices had been replaced by the gleaming wetness of her own saliva.

'Good. Then we can proceed. Simone.'

Simone took hold of Andrea's arm and pulled her to her feet, her fingers deliberately pinching into her flesh. Like Sophia, she took evident pleasure in making sure the slaves were not given an easy time. She walked her to the middle of the room, then reached up above her head and pulled down a nylon rope hanging from a pulley attached to a wooden beam that traversed the ceiling. She attached the rope to the central link of the padded leather cuffs around Andrea's wrists. Andrea felt a familiar pulse of sensation deep inside her sex. Since she had first met Charles she had been bound in numerous positions, but the more tightly she was restrained the more her body seemed to respond with overwhelming floods of feeling.

Simone had taken a long tubular metal bar from an ornate walnut chest of drawers. Andrea knew what it was for. A leather cuff was attached to each end of the metal. Simone knelt at her feet and buckled one of the cuffs around Andrea's left ankle.

'Spread your legs,' she ordered.

Andrea obeyed. But she didn't spread them far enough apart to accommodate the length of the bar and the girl slapped the inside of her thigh painfully.

'Wider,' she chided.

With Andrea's legs splayed wide she strapped the other cuff in place, making it impossible for Andrea to close them again.

Was it her imagination or could she feel the lips of her sex, already sticky with the sweet sap of her excitement, parting too? The feeling of being bound and spread like this, completely vulnerable, exposed and helpless, made every nerve in her body hum.

Marie-Claire walked over to the wall where the other end of the rope was tied off to a brass cleat. She unwound the rope and pulled it through the pulley. As the rope was raised Andrea's wrists were hauled up too, forcing her to bend forward. When her torso was at right angles to her legs and her arms were pulled up behind her almost vertically, Marie-Claire tied the rope off to the cleat again.

The pain in her arms and shoulders was acute. Andrea groaned, trying to twist into a more comfortable position, but the bondage was too tight to allow anything but the most minuscule of movements. She was intensely aware of her sex, her labia and the mouth of her vagina laid open. She could feel a trickle of juices escaping the silky wet flesh.

She tried to raise her head but the cramp in her neck made the effort too painful. Marie-Claire walked up behind her. One hand smoothed over the lush curves of Andrea's buttocks, then slid between her legs.

Andrea felt the fingers spreading her labia further apart. Two entered her vagina so forcefully that she tried to rear up in protest, though her bondage did not allow her to get far. She could feel Marie-Claire's rings, cold and sharp, against her melting flesh. The French woman drove her fingers forward and twisted them, while a third finger butted against the perfectly circular hole of Andrea's anus. Not a day had passed at the chateau without some special attention being paid to this part of her anatomy. Every single night she had been made to sleep with a large dildo strapped into it. She had been trained to hold items there, each day the objects getting progressively heavier. And Pierre, Marie-Claire's husband, had used her exclusively in the rear, his cock larger than any of the dildos they'd applied. When his phallus swelled as he ejaculated she'd thought it would split her in two. This treatment had left the little orifice sore, and it tingled as Marie-Claire wriggled her fingernail against it.

'Not so tight now, I think,' she said pensively. She withdrew her fingers from Andrea's vagina and thrust them into her anus. Fortunately the copious juices from Andrea's sex lubricated their passage, but nevertheless she winced at this sudden intrusion. Just as they had in her vagina, the fingers twisted and turned, exploring intimately. And just like her vagina, her anus responded with a whole flood of feeling.

Suddenly the fingers were withdrawn. 'Over here, Patrick, at once,' Marie-Claire commanded.

Patrick shuffled over to her on his knees, knowing better than to get to his feet without being ordered to.

'I want you to use your tongue on her, Patrick. We have been training her all week to make sure she has control of her desires, and I need to test how far she has come.'

'Yes, madam.'

Patrick crawled between Andrea's legs. She could feel his hot breath playing over her labia.

Marie-Claire caught hold of his hair and forced his face into Andrea's sex. His nose slid into the mouth of her labia.

'Does that feel good?'

'Mmmm...' His reply was muffled by Andrea's sex. She felt his tongue moving up to her clit.

The training she had received during the last two months had comprised of two distinct strands. The first had been endless schooling to improve her physical capabilities. As with the exercises she had been given for her anus, her labia and her vagina had been developed in the same way, the interior muscles of her sex made to contract as she was penetrated over and over again. She had been made to exercise her tongue, enabling her to extend it further and use it for longer periods, and be more limber by performing yoga-like movements, designed no doubt to increase her ability to spread herself open and offer herself to her masters. Any infractions, even the slightest hesitation or delay, had been punished with the whip or the cane.

But the arduous repetitions that were enforced on her in this daily grind were nothing compared to what she had been subjected to at night. The second strand of her education was designed to put the exercises to good use. After being showered, elaborately made-up and dressed in some outre garment, like the one she was wearing now, she had been taken upstairs. Either in the training block or in the main house every night without exception she'd been bound so tightly so could not move, and instructed that under no circumstances was she allowed to come. Then either Marie-Claire or her husband, or one or both of the girls - and sometimes all four of them - had used every means in their power to accomplish that very goal. Standing spread-eagled across a vertical frame two nights ago, for instance, she had been buggered by Pierre while his wife penetrated her vagina with a large and powerful vibrator and Sophia and Simone plied her nipples, using their fingers and their mouths to tease and torment them. The bondage alone, her ankles and wrists bound by leather cuffs attached to short chains at each corner of the frame, had been enough to set Andrea's body alight, and the desire to orgasm as she had felt Pierre's rigid cock thrusting slowly into her bottom, had been irresistible. But she knew she had to resist. Her orgasm was in the gift of her master. Only when a master gave permission was a slave allowed to come, and she had to learn control. Absolute control. Marie-Claire had made it very clear that exceptions would not be tolerated. If Andrea wanted to be a slave and serve her master she would have to learn the hard way.

Patrick's tongue nudged against her clitoris. Andrea moaned softly. Tied like this, the pain of the acute bondage already turning into that most peculiar but keenest of pleasures, her sexual nerves had been set on edge. If she wriggled her bottom from side to side ever so slightly, rubbing her clit against Patrick's tongue, it would be more than enough to bring her off. But that was the reverse of what she must do. She had no idea what Marie-Claire intended for her in this latest test, but she was sure that this was only the beginning.

'Come on, I want to see some action,' demanded Marie-Claire.

Andrea heard the unique sound of a whip thwacking against flesh. She guessed Marie-Claire was using it to encourage Patrick's endeavours.

Immediately his tongue dragged across Andrea's clitoris. The corded nerves bunched in the little button of flesh reacted sharply. He repeated the same manoeuvre several times then used the very tip of his tongue to burrow up under her clitoris. This again produced a huge wave of delight. It was as if he'd found the most sensitive spot on her entire body.

'He's good at it, no?' Marie Claire said.

'Y-yes,' Andrea gasped.

'This is little Patrick's speciality. He is not a slave. He comes to me to be treated like one, and in return he tests my girls for me. Sophia and Simone adore him.'

The tongue seemed to be boring into her like a drill. Her whole body began to tremble.

'You must not come,' Marie-Claire reminded her. 'Simone, why don't you come over here and join in. You know how sensitive Andrea's tits are. Why don't you work on them for her.'

'No...' Andrea protested weakly.

'*Bien sure*,' Simone said.

Andrea saw her legs appear at her side. Her hands wrapped around her back and cupped her breasts, then pressed them back against her chest, making the nipple clips bite again, the numbness instantly forgotten.

Andrea was consumed with a pain so laced with intense pleasure that it was impossible to distinguish the two. She could feel her orgasm gathering, like a huge wave held back by a flimsy dam. She knew she must not allow the dam to be breached, but that in itself only made matters worse. It was a vicious circle.

The more her body was tortured by the need to hold back the more that torture contributed to her growing need to come. Marie-Claire was right. She was a masochist.

'Enough,' Marie-Claire said suddenly.

Patrick stopped. With huge relief Andrea felt his face moving away.

Her relief was short-lived. 'Blindfold her, and a gag.'

'No!'

That was the worst. Being deprived of the ability to see focussed everything inward. In the blackness there was nothing to do but concentrate on what she was feeling. The gag too, being forcibly silenced, only heightened her excitement.

'Yes,' Marie-Claire insisted.

Simone took a silk blindfold and a gag from the chest of drawers. She came back to Andrea and bent over, carefully placing the padded silk over her eyes, then stretching the elasticated straps around the back of her head. Andrea was plunged into darkness.

She felt something being pressed against her lips. It smelt strongly of rubber. She opened her mouth and felt a long wedge-shaped object penetrating it, the thinner end pressing right back to her throat, the wider stretching her lips apart. The wedge was attached to a leather strap that Simone secured around the back of her neck.

A finger smeared something cold and creamy down between her buttocks, massaging it in.

'*Bon. Maintenait, Patrick l'enculer.*'

'*Oui, madam.*'

Andrea heard him getting to his feet. As he did the knob of his cock nudged against her leg just above the welt of the black stocking. His belly rested against her bottom, making the weals sting as his cock slid into the cleft of her buttocks, nosing down to the little crater of her anus.

In her mind's eye she could see the dark red rubber-bound glans pulsing as it pressed into the puckered hole. She tried to open for him as she'd been so vigorously trained to do. He stabbed forward. There was no resistance, the cream lubricating his passage. Andrea felt a rush of sensation as his erection thrust deeply into her most private place.

There was no doubt that Marie-Claire's training had been effective. When her master had buggered her for the first time the pain had overwhelmed her. And so had the intensity of the pleasure that kicked in seconds later. Now things were different. There was pain, but it was much less pronounced. And the pleasure was different too. Her anus seemed to have become sensitised, able to deliver pleasure not only by virtue of translated pain, but in its own right and almost as keenly as her vagina.

She found herself sucking on the gag, using it as if it were a cock, wanting to feel two phalluses inside her. But she stopped herself at once as both her mouth and her bottom delivered a double hit of concentrated pleasure, an arc of electricity connecting the two and lighting up everything along its path. Desperately she tried to claw herself back to some semblance of control, but in the darkness, unable to see anything but the images of sex that flickered in her mind, it was incredibly difficult.

She groaned into the gag. Simone's hands were back. This time they were fishing inside the basque. Andrea knew at once what they were doing. She felt persistent fingers on the nipple clips. The reaction of the poor buds, trapped and numbed for so long, to being released was much greater than the initial pain. If she wasn't very careful that alone would take her over the edge.

She tried to think of something to hold herself back. She tried to think of Charles Darrington Hawksworth, looking at her sternly, his cold blue eyes unblinking and unemotional. Simone's fingers opened the left-hand clip and a huge jolt of sensation ratcheted through Andrea's body. It seemed to be routed directly to her clit, which pulsed wildly. Her anus too clenched around the rock hard phallus that was sliding slowly in and out.

But she managed to hang on. The second clip was released and a second wave ran through her. But somehow, she would never know quite how, she managed to hold herself back. The training, the hours of torment, had had their effect.

'Could you feel that?' Marie-Claire asked Patrick.

'God yes,' Patrick said, forgetting himself for a moment. Then he quickly used the proper form of address, 'Yes, madam.'

'Ready for more?' This question was addressed to Andrea.

Andrea shook her head as vigorously as she could. She was trembling, every nerve stretched and strained. She had never wanted to orgasm more in her life.

'Oh yes, you are,' Marie-Claire said.

Andrea felt Simone's hands move away from her breasts. That was a little relief, but only temporary. Almost immediately she felt something cold and greasy being nosed into the top of her labia. It butted against her clitoris, causing a jolt of sensation, then pushed down to the mouth of her vagina. Her soft lips were already wide open and the object sunk between them, pushing into her cunt.

She screamed, though only a muffled sound escaped the gag.

The feeling of having two large phalluses alongside each other in her body was indescribable. Patrick's cock, hot, wet and animate, throbbed violently as it too reacted to the new intruder, causing it to swell to even greater proportions inside her bottom. Now every region of her body was being stimulated, every erogenous zone except her breasts, being assailed by the most wonderful sensations. And Marie-Claire did not leave her breasts for long. Seconds after the dildo had been thrust into her vagina Andrea felt a hand folding back the bra of the basque and a mouth reaching up to suck at her tenderised nipples. It pinched the left between its teeth while long fingernails bit into the right.

Andrea shuddered. How could she possibly resist the feelings that affected every part of her? She tried to twist away but the cruel bondage held her firm, only reminding her of her position. She could see herself as clearly as if she had been looking in a mirror, swathed in black and red satin, her legs sheathed in glossy black nylon, her arms held vertical and her legs spread open by the metal bar. It was an image that reached deep into her psyche, stirring all the long buried desires that had so recently been unearthed.

'Now make him come,' Marie-Claire ordered, firmly but quietly.

'No please...' Patrick said. 'Please madam, not with the preventer on. I've been good; I've done everything you've said.'

His plea must have worked. Had he been a slave of course such behaviour would have resulted in a severe punishment, but Andrea felt him being pulled out of her bottom and heard a snap of rubber as the little helmet that had restrained him so effectively was pulled off.

Andrea was so close to the brink she felt as though she was suspended in mid-air, but had not yet fallen down the precipice. But Marie-Claire's new command saved her. She had something to concentrate on now, putting all her training, all her endless exercises, into practice.

As Patrick's unfettered cock again slid into her rear, Andrea used her internal muscles to grip him. It must have been effective because she heard him groan loudly. This is what Marie-Claire had taught her. Men could be milked - milked of their spunk. She relaxed her hold and pushed back at him as hard as her bonds would allow, then clenched her anus tightly around him again.

There had to be a rhythm. Grip and release. Grip and release. Each time she gripped a huge wave of pleasure threatened to derail her efforts, but she managed to hold on. She seemed to be able to feel every inch of his cock, the distinct ridge at the base of the glans, even the veins that gnarled his long shaft. It was pulsing as wildly as it had when Simone had pushed the vibrator into her vagina, swelling against the narrow tube in which it was so tightly enclosed. Surely he could not resist for much longer.

Andrea used every last ounce of energy to squeeze his cock again. This time she didn't release it, but held on as strongly as she could and ground her hips from side to side.

Patrick groaned loudly. Suddenly his cock jerked upward and Andrea felt a boiling fluid gushing into her bottom.

'Now you,' Marie-Claire said. 'I give you

permission.' As she spoke her teeth gnawed into Andrea's nipple again.

Andrea twisted in her bondage, wanting to feel the restraints. The pain that exploded in her tortured muscles, and that peculiar pleasure that followed it, took her over the top and plunged her into an orgasm, the nerves in her anus, her vagina, her clit and her nipples on fire; a consuming fire that spread through her body. If it had not been for the gag she would have been screaming. As it was she heard only a low long keening noise.

She collapsed, with no energy to support herself any more, her body hanging limply from the pulley above her head. She felt her anus expel Patrick's softening cock. That made her shudder.

'*Quelle domage*,' Marie-Claire said. 'It looks as though you are ready, *ma cherie*. It seems it's time I let you go.'

Chapter 2

Andrea fitted her arms into the spaghetti straps of the black silk slip then allowed it to shimmer down her torso. She was already wearing a lacy black bra, a pair of matching thong cut panties and a thin suspender belt supporting flesh-coloured stockings.

Moving without any form of restraint, without manacles at her ankles or leather cuffs strapped tightly around her wrists, gave her the feeling that she was floating. She had got so used to the little jerks and sharp yanks of her bondage, that they had become second nature to her. She had learnt to undertake every physical activity slowly and carefully and to make sure she did nothing spontaneously. Spontaneity, sudden unplanned movements, inevitably produced nips of pain.

Andrea picked up the black skirt of the suit Marie-Claire had given her and stepped into it. It was tight and barely covered the tops of her stockings. She smoothed the material out over her bottom, then put on the jacket. There was no blouse and even with the jacket fully buttoned it revealed more than a hint of the plunging front of the slip and the bra underneath, her breasts moulded together by the silky lingerie.

She looked at herself in the mirror. That too afforded quite a contrast. Whatever outfit she had been made to wear over the past weeks it had never been as modest as this. Invariably the leather, rubber, satin or silk garments she had been squeezed or strapped into had left her breasts, her buttocks or her sex bare, and frequently a combination of all three. Now only her shadowy cleavage gave any hint of immodesty.

'Ready?' The door had opened and Marie-Claire strode in. She was wearing a mid-thigh length black velvet dress with a dropped waist and long black velvet gloves.

'Yes, madam,' Andrea answered.

'Good.' Marie-Claire took two steps toward her and stroked her cheek very gently with the back of a gloved hand. 'Your master will be pleased.'

'Will I see him again?'

'That is entirely up to him. Now follow me.'

They walked upstairs. As they walked towards the front door of the chateau a black car with opaque windows swept up the large circular driveway. Its tyres threw up a little gravel as it came to a halt.

Sophia was standing by the front door. At a sign

from Marie-Claire she opened it, then opened the rear passenger door of the car. She peered inside. 'Out,' she said.

A moment later a long-haired blonde emerged. She was naked apart from bright elaborately laced red patent leather ankle boots and a thick collar of the same material. Running from the front of the collar, down between her small breasts, was a long narrow strap. It cut deeply into her thickly haired sex then emerged to run all the way up her spine, joining the collar again at the back. Her wrists were strapped behind her in leather cuffs and the narrow strap was threaded through the central link of these cuffs. Metal manacles were clipped around her ankles and were joined by an extremely short chain, making it impossible for the girl to take anything other than the smallest steps.

'Welcome to the chateau,' Marie-Claire said as she led Andrea out of the house.

'Get me out of these fucking straps,' the girl screamed, squirming from side to side in a useless attempt to get free. Her accent was American.

Andrea glimpsed something between her legs. It looked as if the tightness of the narrow red strap was being used to keep a flared black dildo crammed tightly into her anus.

'My dear, such an attitude is only going to make your life here extremely unpleasant.'

'You fucking bitch, get me out of this.' The American tried to twist her hands around in front of her but as she did so she lost her balance and crashed down onto her side on the gravel.

'I think this one is going to need some very special attention, don't you Sophia?'

Sophia smiled, obviously enjoying the prospect of

having another victim to torment. 'Yes, madam. Very much so.'

'Take her inside. We'll begin immediately.'

Sophia stooped and picked the girl up. For a moment the fall seemed to have taken the girl's spirit away and she allowed the gravel that stuck to her flesh to be brushed off, walking meekly into the house, the manacles biting into her ankles as she took tiny steps.

'Goodbye, Andrea,' Marie-Claire said, turning back to her. 'Don't let me down. Remember everything I have taught you.'

'Yes, madam, I'll try,' Andrea said. She had no idea what was going to happen to her next, and knew it was no good trying to ask. She hoped she was being returned to Charles Darrington Hawksworth, even though she had reconciled herself to the fact that he would send her away to a new master. He had no choice. That was how *The System* worked. But the thought of seeing Charles again, however briefly, made her pulse quicken.

Marie-Claire led her over to the car and she got inside. The car door closed and the engine purred into life. Minutes later it was heading down the long carriage driveway.

The driver was separated from the passenger compartment by a glass partition that remained firmly shut. Like the car windows the partition was opaque, and Andrea could not clearly see the driver.

It took about an hour to reach the airport, the same airport she had arrived at with Charles Hawksworth some two weeks before. The car swept into a private entrance and parked by a white Lear jet. Immediately a smart young brunette appeared from the plane. She walked up to the car and opened the passenger door.

'Andrea?' she asked.

Andrea nodded.

'Good. Get out of the car please. Everything's being done in rather a rush. I'm Laurie Angelis,' she continued as Andrea accepted her proffered hand and slipped out of the vehicle. 'You're now officially under my control. Until the disposal. Do you understand?'

'No,' Andrea said honestly.

'You address me as Ms Angelis.'

'No, Ms Angelis.'

'Didn't Marie-Claire explain the procedure? That's the trouble with that woman - she's no respect for *The System*. Anyway, you are expected to obey me exactly as you obeyed her. That's what your master demands. What are you wearing under the suit?' Laurie was probably in her mid-thirties and wore a beige-coloured safari suit with a knee length shirt. Her very black hair was cut short in layers and she wore large gold earrings.

'A slip, a bra...'

'Stockings?' The girl decided to see for herself, pulling the tight skirt up until she glimpsed the stockings tops. 'Black lace lingerie?'

'Yes.'

'Are you pierced, tits or labia?'

'No.

'That'll have to do. We need to get you on camera. The disposal is tomorrow and the tapes need to go out today. Come on, follow me.'

The brunette led the way up into the plane. The main cabin was long and narrow with two armchairs and a leather sofa. There was a bar at one end with three barstools bolted to the floor.

'Kneel down,' Laurie said, turning and heading

towards the flight deck.

Andrea knelt on the thickly carpeted floor. Nothing that Laurie had said helped her work out what was going to happen next.

The outer doors of the plane closed and the engines began to roar. There was a loud thump from the undercarriage and the plane began to taxi forward very slowly.

Laurie appeared in the cabin again.

'All right, take that suit off.' She walked to the bar and picked up a shiny metal briefcase from behind it. As Andrea began to pull off her clothes the brunette took out a video camera. With what was obviously practised ease she set it up on a tripod, so the lens was pointing at Andrea.

The captain announced that they were about to take off and should fasten their seatbelts.

'Stay where you are,' Laurie said. She knelt by Andrea's side and wrapped a heavy belt made from the same nylon webbing used for seatbelts tightly around Andrea's legs just above her knees, clenching it so securely the material dug into her flesh. She secured another length of webbing around her ankles. Laurie then took a heavy-duty steel cable, hooking one end into the floor of the cabin behind Andrea's feet, then drawing it between her thighs and up over the strap at her knees, and securing it into the floor a foot or so in front of Andrea, making it impossible for her to stand up. Quickly, the girl got to her feet.

'Hands above your head.'

There was another harness hanging from the bulkhead; a pair of metal manacles attached to a steel cable. Laurie clipped the manacles around Andrea's wrists, then adjusted the cable so her arms were held vertically above her and she was stretched taut.

'That'll hold you nice and secure,' Laurie said, strapping herself into the nearest leather armchair.

As the plane began to accelerate along the runway, Laurie kicked off one of her shoes. Andrea was still wearing the lacy black slip. Laurie's toes climbed Andrea's body until they reached her fleshy breasts. The sudden and unexpected bondage had already created an all too familiar tingling of arousal in Andrea, and as Laurie's foot butted against her nipple she gasped, looking directly into the girl's eyes.

The plane took off. Laurie pressed the sole of her foot against Andrea's breast, until her nipple was being crushed against her ribcage. Then she moved it over to the other breast and did the same. Her hand moved up under her own skirt. Andrea saw her fingers delving down between her thighs. She was wearing white panties and tan-coloured hold up stockings.

'Mmm...' she murmured, as a finger rubbed the white material against her labia. Not satisfied with this she spread her legs apart, pushed the gusset of the panties aside and slid the finger down into her sex. 'Pity there's no time to have you do this for me. I bet you've got a lovely soft mouth.' She moaned as her finger butted against her clit. Her eyes were roaming Andrea's body, her foot still pressed against her aching breast. Andrea saw the muscles of her leg stiffen as she pressed her finger inward, angling it into her vagina.

There was a subtle ping as the seat-belt sign was turned off and the plane banked slightly to the left. Andrea could see the neatly farmed French countryside set out in geometric shapes below.

Laurie snapped her seatbelt open. 'We haven't much time,' she said. She pulled her finger out of her sex and licked it like an ice cream. 'Pity...' She got to her feet and smoothed her skirt down. Stooping over she took hold of the hem of Andrea's black slip and pulled it up until it was clear of her body. 'Hold this, here,' she said, feeding the delicate material into Andrea's fingers.

The brunette unclipped Andrea's bra, allowing her large breasts to spring free. Then she pulled the waistband of the tiny panties down until they banded her thighs. 'That's better,' she said thoughtfully.

She unhooked the phone from its position on the bulkhead and punched a single button. 'All right, I'm ready for you now,' was all she said. Putting the phone back she went to the video camera and, after a few adjustments, started to film the trussed girl.

'Yes, Ms Laurie.' A tall, athletic looking man had appeared from the forward cabin. He was wearing a steward's uniform of black trousers and a white linen jacket.

'I need your help, Eric,' Laurie said.

'Certainly Ms.'

'They have to see her going through her paces. Would you mind?' Laurie tapped the camera by way of explanation.

'Whatever you require, Ms.' Eric immediately unbuttoned his jacket. He threw it aside then pulled off his shoes, socks and trousers. He was wearing a white T-shirt and black briefs, and had hairy muscular limbs.

'This is one of the perks of the job I really enjoy,' he said, grinning broadly as he eased his briefs down.

He was standing directly in front of Andrea and his cock had already begun to engorge. It was large and circumcised and very smooth, the shaft almost as pink as the bulb-shaped glans.

'Suck him, Andrea,' Laurie ordered.

Andrea leant forward and wrapped her lips around the steward's erection. She felt a deep throb of arousal as the rigid shaft slid into her mouth.

'That's good,' Laurie encouraged. 'All the way back, then lick around the glans,' she instructed.

Andrea obeyed, straining forward from her suspended arms.

'All right, you better cut her down for the bottom work,' Laurie suddenly said. 'Strap her arms out front.'

This was clearly not the first time Eric had been brought into service in this way. He unclipped the metal manacles from the overhead cable and pulled Andrea forward by them, clipping them to the same fastening that held the cable that ran between her legs and forcing her forward so her bottom was raised.

'Is that what you want?' he asked.

'Yes... that's good,' Laurie decided.

'And this?' he said. He knelt behind Andrea and took her hips in his hands, immediately directing his cock up between her buttocks.

'Good.' Laurie brought the camera down to floor level. 'Now feed it into her.'

'Cunt first?'

'It doesn't matter.'

Andrea felt Eric's throbbing erection nudging her bottom. With her legs tied so tightly together the position was awkward, and her labia were pursed tightly between her buttocks. But his cock thrust into them and was immediately smeared with her juices.

'She's very eager,' Eric panted.

'Good. Put it all the way in, then pull it out.'

Eric did as he was told. Andrea gasped as his cock slid into her body. It was not possible to push deep in their position, but without being able to open her legs her sex was clenched tightly around him. She didn't understand why, and hadn't from the moment Charles Darrington Hawksworth had first treated her like this, but the more her needs were simply ignored and she was treated merely as an object, the more her body seemed to generate unbelievable waves of yearning.

'I can feel her throbbing,' he said.

'Pull out now.'

The camera lens focussed on Eric's glans as it pulled out of the tight grip of Andrea's vagina. It was glistening wet.

'Okay, now her anus,' Laurie continued directing.

Eric's cock slid up the cleft of Andrea's buttocks. She felt it nudge into the little crater of her arse.

'Like this?' he said, pushing forward. Her anus was closed and dry but Eric used the tip of his glans to smear the lubrication from her sex all over the little opening. He pushed forward. Andrea felt her sphincter resist. With her legs closed it was difficult to apply the training Marie-Claire had instilled.

'She's very tight,' he grunted.

'That's good,' Laurie said enthusiastically from behind the camera. 'They'll like that.' The lens closed on Andrea's buttocks. The bulbous glans was dimpling her bottom, trying to force its way inside.

'That looks good,' Laurie said, focussing the camera into an even tighter close-up.

Suddenly Andrea's anus loosened and Eric's cock sank inside. There was such a sharp explosion of feeling that Andrea yelped. Eric was big and despite Marie-Claire's efforts to enlarge her anus, the pain was intense. But it quickly turned to a wonderful warm pleasure that had Andrea's whole body trembling as she felt the rest of the shaft burying inside her rear. Reflexively her bottom clenched around him.

'Now pull out again.'

Eric did as he was told. He held his glans just outside the little ring of muscles. Andrea felt them contract like a mouth gasping for air.

'That's a great shot,' Laurie said. 'Put it right up inside again.'

Eric grasped Andrea's hips and pushed forward. His erection thrust into her rear passage. She felt her clit pulse wildly and her vagina, empty and unused, yearned for fulfilment.

'Out again.'

The camera lens closed on Andrea's anus as the erect penis pulled slowly out, the round mouth closing back on itself.

'All right, that'll do it,' Laurie said. She turned off the camera. 'Thanks, Eric. This should have been done at the chateau, but you know what Marie-Claire's like. Not very practical.'

'So don't I get my reward?' Eric said sulkily, indicating his large erection.

'And what reward is that?' Laurie said coyly.

'Come on, sweetie. You know you want it too. Bend over the sofa.'

Andrea saw Laurie's eyes flash with excitement. She dropped to her knees in front of Eric and reached up, taking his cock in both hands. While one fingered his scrotum the other fed his shaft into her mouth. She sucked it so hard her cheeks dimpled. 'Oh, she tastes good,' Laurie concluded as she released the pulsing stalk, Andrea's juices on her tongue and lips. She rose and bent over the leather sofa and pulled her skirt up around her waist. She was wearing tan-coloured hold ups and white satin panties. With one hand she pulled the crotch of her panties aside, then wriggled her hips.

Her labia and black pubes were glossy with her excitement. 'Is that what you wanted?' she teased.

Eric didn't need to be asked twice. He caught hold of her hips and thrust his already wet cock into the open maw. It slid right up to the hilt. Andrea saw his balls slapping against Laurie's thighs.

'Mmm...' Laurie cooed dreamily. 'Quite a big boy.' She reached out and touched Andrea's back. Her fingers moved down over her buttocks. 'Pity there isn't time to have you both.'

Eric plunged forward. Andrea saw his fingers clutching at Laurie's hips, digging into the soft flesh. 'Yes,' he grunted triumphantly.

'Can you feel this?' Laurie coaxed. Eric moaned. From the glazed expression on his face it seemed she was gripping him with the muscles of her vagina.

'I coming...' he whispered hoarsely.

'Yes... give it to me.'

Eric thrust forward one more time, pulling Laurie back onto him as he did so. He shuddered and Andrea watched his eyes close and nostrils flare. His hips jerked, his muscular back covered in sweat.

'Jesus,' he gasped, every muscle in his body locked. It was a long time before he opened his eyes and moved again.

The plane banked sharply and turned. Andrea saw the unmistakable landmarks of the London skyline spread out beneath them.

'Ladies and gentleman,' the captain announced over the tannoy. 'Please fasten your seatbelts, we are about to make our final approach to London Heathrow.'

A stretch limousine was waiting as the plane taxied to a halt, its tinted windows reflecting the bright sunlight. As Laurie stooped to undo the steel cable that passed between Andrea's legs the outer door opened with a clunk, a small set of metal steps extending automatically down to the tarmac.

Laurie unclipped the manacles from her wrists too and helped her to her feet. The black slip slithered back down to hug the curves of her torso.

'Come on,' Laurie said.

'What about my clothes?' Andrea asked.

'Now don't tell me you're shy?' Laurie mocked, pulling her to the hatch.

Andrea managed to wrestle the panties up over her hips again as they walked across the tarmac to the car, but her bra still hung loosely from her shoulders.

Laurie opened one of the rear car doors. 'In,' she said unnecessarily.

As she stooped to climb inside Andrea's heart leapt. Sitting in one corner of the leather seat was Charles Darrington Hawksworth. He had his legs crossed and was looking at her steadily, his piercing blue eyes expressing no emotion. 'Good afternoon, my dear,' he said.

There was another woman sitting beside him. She was a striking redhead, her flaming auburn hair forming a halo around her face, with a slender body and rangy legs. She was wearing a white suit and white calf length boots with spiked heels.

'Master,' Andrea breathed.

'Kneel here on the floor,' he said. There was a large expanse of black carpet in the limousine and Andrea slid to her knees in front of him, her pulse racing.

'My God, she did it,' the redhead said in amazement.

'I was anxious to see you again,' he said, ignoring the redhead's remark.

'Thank you, master.' How those words lifted her

spirits.

'The only reason for her to be here is to obey, Karen,' he said, turning to his companion. 'That's what I was trying to explain to you.'

'And she'll do anything?'

'Naturally. All right, Laurie, thank you,' he said, looking over Andrea's shoulder.

Laurie immediately closed the car door, then walked around and got in beside the driver. The car started off across the airport towards a gatehouse, where security guards waved it to halt again.

'So, my dear,' Charles said. 'I've had a very good report from Marie-Claire. She was most impressed.'

'Thank you, master,' said Andrea, trying to suppress her pride.

'And who is Marie-Claire?' the redhead asked.

'Of course, you don't know about *The System*,' Charles said. 'Marie-Claire is responsible for training.'

'Training?'

'Girls like Andrea find it easy enough to express their natural desires and feelings, to behave in a way that is totally submissive. That is fine if they are never going to go into the outside world. But if a master decides to share them, to allow them to be used outside his intimate circle, they must be properly trained.'

'And she agrees to all this?' the redhead persisted, indicating Andrea.

'Naturally. She is a slave, Karen. My slave. She will do anything I ask because that is in her nature - that is what she wants. Isn't that right, Andrea?'

'Yes, master,' Andrea said respectfully.

'And she will obey me, too? She'll do anything I want?'

'As long as I tell her that's what she must do.'

'And will you?' There was an eager glint in the woman's eyes.

'Of course,' he said casually. 'What have you in mind?'

The car had apparently cleared the security checks. The chain link gates were opened and the driver set off along a slip road that led to a dual carriageway. Soon the car had joined the stream of fast moving traffic.

'I'm not sure,' admitted the woman, after drinking in the enticingly submissive vision of Andrea for a while. 'I've never seen anyone like her before.'

'That's why I brought you along, my dear. I thought it would amuse you.'

'There's something about those eyes,' continued the redhead, her attention focussed avidly on Andrea so that she seemed not to hear his words. 'Seeing her like that, so submissive, it makes me feel hot. Is that what you want from me?' she asked him. 'Kneeling in my underwear, waiting to obey you?'

Charles laughed. 'I hardly think you're the type, do you Karen? I thought a more dominant role might suit you. Not all women are submissives. Far from it. Some of those in *The System* are women, and most have women overseers. Like Laurie.' He nodded towards the brunette in the front seat. 'That might be a role that interests you a great deal more.'

'You sound as if you're trying to recruit me,' noted the redhead.

'*Interest* you would be a better word,' he countered. 'Of course, there are always vacancies...'

'And you?'

'I find it amusing to watch. So be my guest.'

'I just tell her what to do?'

Charles nodded.

Karen leant forward, a little uncertainly, examining Andrea's body with new interest. Andrea had seen that look before. It was a deep-rooted excitement combined with an air of scepticism, as if not quite believing the power that had been gifted.

'Come closer,' Karen said, her husky voice betraying her emotion. 'Kneel in front of me.'

Andrea inched forward on her knees.

'Pull your slip up,' the redhead ordered.

Andrea did as she was told. The black slip caught on the unfastened bra and pulled that up too, revealing her breasts.

'Take it off, the bra too,' Karen went on.

Andrea pulled both garments over her head.

'Mmm... quite lovely,' the woman said. She turned to Charles. 'I think I'd like to watch her playing with herself.'

'You only have to ask her, my dear,' he prompted quietly.

Karen raised a foot. Tentatively she pushed the white leather toe of the boot against Andrea's nearest breast, moving it until the tip of the toe was nudging against her nipple.

'Kiss it,' she whispered firmly.

There was no doubt what 'it' meant. Andrea took hold of Karen's heel and kissed the leather boot.

'And the other one.'

Clearly Karen had no intention of moving her other foot, which remained on the carpeted floor so Andrea had to lean down and plant her lips on the leather.

'So obedient,' Karen said, almost to herself. 'Now suck on the heel.'

She lifted, presenting Andrea with a clear view up her long legs. She was wearing pale stockings and

Andrea could see the creamy contours of her thighs, and the gusset of silky red panties pulled tight. The sight made her clitoris pulse longingly.

'Come on,' Karen urged impatiently.

Andrea sucked on the spiked heel, her eyes locked on the woman's vulva. The red panties had folded into the slit of Karen's sex and Andrea could see the outline of her puffy labia.

'Have you ever enjoyed another woman before?' Charles asked.

'Yes... but not like this,' Karen breathed, her growing excitement clearly evident. She dropped her foot and pressed it up between Andrea's thighs. She reached forward and cupped the soft breast she'd been massaging with her boot, cupping it, then pinching the nipple. 'It must be extraordinary...' she said pensively, '...no decisions to make, no responsibilities...'

'You sound envious,' Charles said.

'No.' Karen shuddered. 'But I can understand its attractions. All she has to do is obey. That is reducing life to a wonderfully simple equation.'

'Exactly.'

Very slowly Karen moved right to the edge of the sumptuous seat. She stroked one fingertip over Andrea's moist lower lip, then pushed it into her mouth. 'Suck it,' she ordered.

Andrea did as she was told. The redhead had long fingers with beautifully manicured fingernails. She sucked on the finger as sensuously as she could. She felt Karen shudder again.

Karen pulled her finger away. A trail of saliva fell onto Andrea's chin.

'I want to see you touch yourself,' Karen said, her voice low and husky. 'I want to see you come. Will you do that for me?'

Andrea looked at Charles. He was smiling indulgently. 'Yes, mistress,' she replied.

'Turn around then.'

Andrea turned on her knees, so she was facing the front of the car, and opened her legs. She knew the black silk gusset of the panties would be pulled tautly over the plane of her sex, and that Karen and Charles would be able to see every detail, her labia outlined under the material. Laurie had twisted around in the front passenger seat and was watching intently too.

Andrea pulled the gusset of her panties aside. The sudden kiss of air between her legs made her labia tingle. She was already wet. She moved her knees further apart and raised a hand, stroking one finger up into her labia so they were pressed apart. Andrea felt her vagina open.

'Concentrate on your clit,' Karen said.

Andrea ran her finger up to the fourchette and found her swollen clitoris. It responded immediately. She brought her other hand around over her buttock and down. With the tips of two and then three fingers she explored the mouth of her vagina, stretching the flesh by scissoring her fingers apart. She wanted them to see inside, the scarlet flesh glistening with her juices.

'Come on, I want to see you come,' Karen said irritably.

Andrea frotted her finger hard over the top of her clit. A second wave of pleasure cascaded through her body. Glistening juices made a trail down her thighs to the stocking tops. She was very close to coming. The idea that she was with her master again, his eyes watching every move she made, excited her more than anything else. She had imagined that he was watching her the whole time she was at the chateau. The image had been so strong she was often surprised when she opened her eyes to find he wasn't there. But now he was. Now that quizzical expression she remembered so well, one eyebrow raised ever so slightly higher than the other, was focussed on her again. Whatever his motives, whatever he planned for Karen, it didn't matter. All that mattered was that her master wanted to be there with her.

Andrea tensed. Her finger was a blur as it moved over her clit. Not wanting to tease herself any more she pushed the fingers of her other hand deep into her cunt, two and then three fingers thrust into her warm tight flesh. She twisted them around, screwing them as deep as they would go, then felt her sex clench tightly around them. 'Oh *God*...' she moaned.

'Do it,' Karen encouraged, her voice heavily laced with excitement.

Andrea ironed a finger against her clitoris, pressing it against the underlying bone as her orgasm leapt through her, a throbbing rhythm that made her vagina spasm too. She moaned, her body trembling.

Karen stared, open-mouthed. She looked at Charles, her eyes wide, her body quivering almost as much as Andrea's.

'And there's more where that came from,' he said, smiling.

'I'm on fire,' Karen said huskily.

'And what do you want to do about it?' he asked, matter-of-factly.

The car had driven through an open gate into a semi-circular driveway of a large Victorian house that Andrea had never seen before. It parked by the porch that protected the front door, its side panels inlaid with stained glass.

Karen did not answer his question.

'Laurie, take the girls inside, will you?' Charles

requested. 'It appears Karen here has a little unfinished business.'

Once inside the house Karen, to Andrea's complete surprise, grabbed her hand and pulled her up the long straight flight of stairs. There was a door at the top to the left, and Karen pushed it open. 'In here,' she said. It was a small guestroom with patterned wallpaper and a dark blue counterpane on the bed.

Karen slammed the door shut in her eagerness to get to grips with the scantily clothed beauty in her grasp. She took Andrea in her arms and kissed her passionately, mashing their lips together. Andrea felt her tongue, persistent and wet, exploring her mouth hungrily, worming around inquisitively. Her hands were all over Andrea's body, caressing her back and buttocks, squeezing her breasts.

'Oh *Christ*,' she shuddered. She pulled away and tore off her white suit jacket. She stripped off the skirt and quickly pulled off the white leather boots and her stockings. Her red panties and bra followed. She threw them aside, her naked body lush and creamy, the marks her underwear had left banding her flesh.

'Get on the bed,' she ordered. But before Andrea could obey Karen caught hold of her arms and dragged her over to the double bed, pushing her back onto the counterpane. Kneeling beside her, she kissed Andrea again before moving her lips down Andrea's exposed throat, nipping and sucking on her flesh. She sucked her nipples while hungrily mauling her breasts. But this didn't last long, for her hands abandoned the luscious flesh and moved down over Andrea's hips as her mouth delved lowered, her tongue licking at Andrea's flat belly. Andrea felt her thighs being prised apart.

For a second Karen paused, staring down into

Andrea's open sex, the crotch of the panties hitched up out of the way, her labia parted, her vagina open, her juices smeared on her thighs. Then she dipped her head and planted her mouth firmly on Andrea's labia, sucking eagerly, her tongue darting inside to find her clit.

'Ooooh...' Andrea moaned as the woman's tongue teased her. At the same time she felt Karen's fingers playing at the mouth of her vagina just as hers had done in the car minutes before. They stretched the labia this way and that, teasing the flesh while her tongue flicked at Andrea's clit.

Suddenly she swung a thigh over Andrea and pushed back until poised above her face. Andrea found herself staring up into the woman's sex. Then, as she pushed her face down between Andrea's thighs again, she settled on Andrea's mouth, squirming so her juices smeared her imprisoned face.

'Yesss...' she hissed, the noise muffled by Andrea's thighs.

They were joined. The heat and wetness of Andrea's sex was penetrated by Karen's tongue. At the same time she felt the melting softness of Karen's sex pressed heavily onto her mouth. Together they prodded and probed each other. Their fingers explored. Together their anuses, sticky from the abundant juices that coated every part of their vulvas, were penetrated, fingers buried in both tunnels.

Andrea was coming from the moment Karen's mouth fastened to her sex, but she knew Karen had come even faster, her body shuddering as she pressed obsessively against Andrea's mouth. But her first orgasm was only the beginning. She came over and over, gluing her mouth to Andrea's sex as Andrea did the same to her.

They were glistening with perspiration. In the sea of lust there were brief moments of calm before Karen's needs reasserted themselves and she swung into action once more, sucking Andrea, her fingers plucking at her breasts, or penetrating her vagina and anus simultaneously, as Andrea reciprocated.

'Quite a performance.'

The voice came as a shock to both of them. They stopped and looked up. Charles Hawksworth was standing in the doorway. He was completely naked and was holding his large erection in one hand and a leather harness and a riding crop in the other.

He walked up to the bed. Eagerly Karen rose to her knees and gobbled his turgid penis into her mouth. 'I think it's my turn, don't you?' he said, looking straight into Andrea's eyes.

'Yes, master,' she said. Despite everything Karen had done to her the thought that she was going to be allowed to touch and caress her master made her almost breathless with anticipation.

He reached forward and took her hand. He pulled it up to his mouth and kissed the tips of her fingers tenderly, licking off the juices. 'It's been a long time,' he said.

'Yes, master.' It had been a very long time.

'Well, Karen,' he continued, 'it's time you learnt your next lesson. Put this on her.' He handed her the leather harness. 'Andrea has to be put into bondage. Then you are going to whip her. Have you ever whipped anyone before?'

'No,' Karen said, her voice thick with passion.

'Then it's time you did.'

Chapter 3

She didn't want to wake up. She could still feel the shadow of her master's rampant penis deep in her vagina. It had left an impression in her bottom too, a wonderful soreness that she relished.

In fact, she was sore all over. Her nipples, pinched and bitten, tingled every time the sheet rubbed against them, and her sex felt raw. But Andrea welcomed the discomfort. It was proof that her master had been so captivated by her that he'd been unable to leave her alone. True, he had spent as much time on Karen as he had on her, but that didn't matter. In order to be able to give him the blind obedience she had made herself totally dependent on him for all her needs, which meant she craved his attention like a drug. The more time he spent with her, and the more intimately he treated her, the more she was able to feel a special bond with him. But curiously, the reverse was not true. If he ignored her, as he had in the past, if he did not send for her or appear to want to see her, she felt no less enthralled by him. It meant only that *she* had done something wrong and must work to get back into favour. The psychology of being a perfect slave was complex.

Eventually, with the sun blazing through the curtains on the top floor of the house where Laurie had taken her to sleep, Andrea got out of bed and went into the en suite bathroom. She had a pee and ran a bath. There was no sign of Karen, and when she tried the bedroom door it was locked. That did not surprise her.

She took a long hot bath, washed her hair and used the make-up that had been left in the bedroom. There were no clothes and nothing to do but sit on the bed, but the euphoria of the night with her master was taking a long time to wear off, and Andrea was happy to sit on the bed and daydream.

Of course she still had no idea what Charles intended for her, who her new master would be or where she would be taken, but after last night she was completely unconcerned. Seeing him again had reinforced everything she had felt about him from the moment she'd gone to dinner at his country estate some months before. He was still her master. She was still his slave. If she had any doubts, if she feared that being away from him, being out of his physical presence would loosen the ties she felt, they had been rapidly dispelled. It didn't matter what he wanted of her. Whatever he asked her to do she would do without question.

Meeting Charles Darrington Hawksworth had changed her life. Instinctively he seemed to know what she wanted. Andrea had never thought of herself as someone who was particularly interested in sex. He had encouraged her to explore her sexuality and to her amazement she had discovered things about herself that she would never have guessed in her wildest dreams. Sex, once dull and uninteresting, and very low on her list of priorities, had taken centre stage. From the moment he had made her kneel in front of him, her hands grasped behind her back, her head lowered, she had felt a passion that had simply overwhelmed her. She had no idea why the idea of submission, the image of herself as nothing more than a slave should be so powerful, but there was simply no denying that it was. She had decided there and then that she could not turn her back on it and to explore the opportunity that had been presented to her, no matter where it led.

Which is exactly what she was doing now. At no point in the last weeks had she been prevented from returning to her old life, but apart from the crisis she'd experienced when Charles had first taken her to Marie-Claire, she had not even been tempted to do it. The training had been arduous and punishing. But it had taught her one valuable lesson: though her devotion to her master was absolute, and no one would ever be able to take his place, being with Marie-Claire and obeying her and her husband's every whim had shown her that the idea of submission, of being a slave, excited and aroused her no matter who was in charge. She had thought she would never be able to respond as unequivocally to another master. It appeared she was wrong. As much as she thought of Charles as her master it appeared that she did not need his physical presence to feel the sort of excitement his commands generated. Her devotion to him was absolute, but not exclusive. As long as she knew he had given his permission, as long as she could picture his stern eyes staring at her with pride, she had learned that the act of submission itself was what excited her, not the person to whom she submitted.

Of course, she was curious as to what her new master would be like, but as she thought about it she realised quite unexpectedly that whoever he was she would be able to accept him. But more than that, the idea of going to a new and completely unknown master had begun to excite her. One day she supposed the adventure would come to an end, she suspected as quickly as if someone had turned off a switch. One day she would no longer want to obey without question. The bondage and pain that was the inevitable corollary of her submission would no longer excite her. But that day had not yet dawned.

She had no idea what time it was. Judging from the light outside the window it must be approaching midday.

Then the door opened and Laurie Angelis appeared. 'Good afternoon,' she said. 'I gather you had a late night.' She was wearing skin-tight black satin jeans and a loose-fitting white top, and was holding a long thin whip with a brass pommel, the lash of the whip tapering away. Andrea could see she was not wearing a bra, her firm breast moving unhindered within the white top and the enticing outline of her puckered nipples pressing against the material.

'Put these on,' she said, dropping some garments on the bed. 'I see you've done your make-up. I'll be back for you in a short while.'

Laurie was about to leave the room again when she seemed to change her mind. 'On the other hand, it seems I was the only one who didn't get a bit of you last night,' she said, sitting on the single bed. 'Perhaps I'll stay and watch.' She tapped the whip against her thigh.

Andrea picked up the clothes. The lingerie consisted of a small bikini bra of black satin, its cups so small they barely covered Andrea's breasts, and matching G-string panties. Both the panties and the bra had delicately embroidered circular holes set in the material, the two in the bra allowing Andrea's nipples to poke through, the one in the panties revealing her blonde pubes. There was a pair of very glossy hold up stockings too, with wide black lace welts.

Andrea quickly pulled on the flimsy items, the black satin moulding to her curves like a second skin. She felt a pulse of arousal as she rolled the stockings up her long legs, the sleek material encasing them tightly.

The dress was black. At first Andrea thought it was fairly conventional with a high neck and long sleeves. It was only as she pulled it on that she realised the front of it was made entirely from transparent black chiffon, as was the material covering her bottom. Only the top half of the back and the long sleeves were made from more conventional black velvet. There was a zip in the chiffon running all the way down the front from throat to hem.

'Very pretty,' Laurie appraised sparingly. 'And very revealing.'

It certainly was. The chiffon hid little. Andrea could see her nipples poking through the bra, the black satin panties and her creamy white thighs above the lacy welts of the stockings. At the back, where only a thin ribbon of black satin emerged from the cleft of her buttocks, her whole bottom would be exposed. There were shoes too, black patent leather high heels with the customary four inch heel, a narrow strap running around the ankle.

'Well,' Laurie said, glancing at her watch, 'it appears we've got a little time to kill. What shall we do?' She smiled and rose smoothly. She kicked off her shoes, unzipped the satin jeans and pulled them down her legs. She was not wearing tights or panties and her sex was shaved and perfectly smooth. She had a small blue tattoo at the top of her thighs in the shape of a coiled snake. 'I want you to do exactly as I tell you,' she said. 'Do you understand?'

'Yes, Ms Angelis,' Andrea replied. The sight of Laurie's body excited her. Before meeting Charles, Andrea had never even imagined having sex with another woman; now, though she had been forced to take women on equal terms with men many times, it still represented an element of the forbidden, a reminder of just how far she had come. That gave it an extra thrill.

'Get to your knees,' Laurie said.

Andrea did as she was told immediately. She found herself staring at Laurie's flat belly. Her pubes had been shaved away and her belly was smooth and hairless.

'Get on with it, then,' Laurie said irritably. 'I don't have to draw you a map, do I?' She wrapped a hand around the back of Andrea's neck and pulled her forward. Andrea kissed the flesh of her belly, feeling her own excitement immediately beginning to mount. She directed her tongue to the pursed labia and ran it between them.

Laurie squirmed her legs further apart. 'Get it right in there,' she directed. 'It's time I had a go at you.' Laurie shuffled forward a few inches until Andrea's body was arched back and her face was forced between her thighs, her face pressed against her sex. She used her tongue, parting Laurie's delicate labia to find her clit. Already her sex was wet, her juices oozing from her vagina. Andrea concentrated on her clit, flicking it from side to side with the tip of her tongue.

'Mmm... nice,' Laurie sighed. 'You're very good at that.' Her fingers dug into the back of Andrea's head, weaving into her long blonde hair. She reached over her shoulder with her other hand and slid open the drawer of the bedside chest. 'Use this,' she said. A small pink dildo, not much bigger than a large finger, appeared between Laurie's thighs. She pushed it up into the mouth of her vagina until she felt Andrea's fingers were holding it securely. Andrea eased it right up into Laurie's cunt, the smooth plastic making a squishy noise as it rode up the tight passage. The dildo was small enough to disappear into Laurie's sex completely, Andrea holding it in place with the tip of her finger.

'Lovely,' Laurie sighed again. 'Use your finger in my arse.'

Andrea wriggled a finger into the cleft of Laurie's buttocks. The hole of her anus was hot and moist. It seemed to be sucking her finger inside.

'Come on,' Laurie urged. She still held the whip and swished it down across Andrea's back.

Andrea twisted her finger into the little hole. She felt the ring of muscles resist, then give way. As her finger was sucked into the tight tube she felt her own anus react as sharply as if it too had been penetrated. Her sex joined in, a spasm deep in her vagina making her moan.

'This is for my benefit, not yours,' Laurie snapped, slapping her with the whip. This time the blow was much stronger, the whip cutting across the top of Andrea's buttocks. 'Get them deeper.'

Andrea screwed her finger up into Laurie's anus as she used her other hand to try and push the little dildo deeper too. She felt Laurie shudder as she flattened her tongue against her clit and dragged it from side to side, allowing her finger and the dildo to slide out a little before she crammed them back in.

'Yessss...' Laurie hissed. 'Do it like that.' She cut the whip down across Andrea's back, ground her sex against Andrea's face and dug the fingers of both hands into Andrea's hair, using it to support herself as her feelings threatened to overwhelm her.

'Yessss...' The word echoed around the small room. Her body quivered as she came, gripping the fingers that penetrated her vagina and her rectum. She opened her legs slightly and wriggled her sex even further down on Andrea's upturned face, wanting to extract every last drop of pleasure, the sticky sap of her body smeared over Andrea's flushed cheeks. Then she gripped her wrists and pulled her hands away, the wet passages of her body making a squelching sound as the dildo and Andrea's fingers were forced out. She held the dildo and brought it up to her lips, sucking it enthusiastically.

'It's a pity we don't have more time,' she said. She picked up the satin jeans and put them back on. 'Come on, we don't want to keep them waiting,' she said, the expression on her face betraying not a hint of the intimacy they had shared.

Downstairs by the front door Andrea was bound. Laurie took a thin but strong and smooth steel chain and wound it around her neck. Attached to the front of the chain was a pair of what looked like miniature handcuffs. Laurie raised Andrea's hands one by one and snapped the little cuffs around her thumbs. There was no more than an inch between the two cuffs so Andrea could not move her hands apart, nor, due to the shortness of the steel chain around her neck, could she straighten her arms again, and had to hold them up against her breasts. The loops of steel that cut into the base of her thumbs were narrow and tight, and immediately made her uncomfortable.

A few minutes later the black stretch limo pulled up outside the front door. There was no sign of Charles, or of Karen for that matter.

'Where are we going?' Andrea asked.

'I thought you knew better than to ask questions,' Laurie admonished.

They walked through the front door and Laurie held the car door open for her. Most of Charles

Hawksworth's properties were surrounded by tall walls or fencing and elaborate security, but the driveway here had nothing more than a low brick wall on the street side, and as Andrea walked to the car a young woman was walking by on the street outside. The sight of Andrea in the bizarre and revealing dress made her stare, the expression on her face turning from disbelief to disgust, but then to what Andrea thought might even be envy.

For twenty or so minutes they drove through North London until the car pulled up in front of a pair of imposing wooden gates, set into a tall brick wall that stretched for some distance in both directions. There was a sign on the gate that read: STRICTLY PRIVATE. Two large men wearing the uniform of a private security firm stood to the right, one with a clipboard in his hand.

There was a faint hum as Laurie operated the switch that wound down the black opaque window on her door. 'Hawksworth,' she announced.

The nearest man consulted his clipboard. 'Party of two,' he confirmed. He examined the interior of the car with a quick glance and then, apparently satisfied, nodded to his colleague, who operated a switch that opened the gates. 'Have a good day,' he said, and waved them on.

The gates swung open silently and Andrea saw a long driveway leading to a large and impressive house set in lavishly planted gardens, the brick wall enclosing the grounds on all sides. There was a large swimming pool and conservatory on one side of the house and a garage block on another. The car drove up to the front door where a man in a black frock coat stood waiting. As the vehicle smoothed to a halt he opened the rear passenger door.

'Good afternoon, Ms Angelis,' he said politely. 'Just one today?'

'Just one,' she answered. 'Is everyone here?' She climbed out of the car and indicated that Andrea should do the same. It was difficult to shift forward with her hands so tightly secured.

'You're the last,' he informed Laurie.

'How many in all?'

'Six.'

Laurie smiled. 'Better get her ready then,' she said.

The man opened the front door and Andrea immediately heard a gabble of voices and the tinkle of glasses. The interior of the house was as luxurious as the exterior, the hall with a deep green carpet and lined with oak panels. There was a display case by the front door containing a huge collection of hatpins; silver, carved ivory and jewelled examples all carefully laid out on red velvet. The walls were hung with oil paintings and some, Andrea recognised, by very expensive artists. There was a large reception room to the right of the hallway and several men and women stood around drinking champagne. One of the men turned and kissed Laurie with exaggerated ceremony on both cheeks. He wore a bright green suit with a canary yellow waistcoat and a yellow and green chequered bow tie.

'Laurie, sweetie, I thought you were bound to be here.' His eyes roamed Andrea's body, the black chiffon hiding little. 'She's pretty,' he said. 'Charles' latest?'

'Of course.'

He took hold of Andrea's arms and lifted them so her elbows were parallel with her chin and he could stare at her breasts, the flesh straining against the little black satin triangles of the bra.

'Nice,' he said, allowing her arms to fall again. 'How long?'

'Oh, don't worry Angus, she's new. But I can't see her attracting your boss. He usually likes the more obvious type. Am I right?'

'Unfortunately,' he agreed. 'He won't touch them unless they've been pierced, and most of them have some ghastly tattoos.'

'I've a tattoo,' Laurie teased.

'I know sweetie, I've seen it. But yours is discreet. Whittaker likes them the size of a dinner plate. And he's taken to having their heads shaved, too. I just don't think all that's a turn on. Something lovely and delicate like her would suit me down to the ground.' His eyes were still firmly fixed on Andrea.

'That's our lot in life, Angus - to pick up the scraps from our master's table.'

'And don't I know it.'

'Is there anyone else interesting?'

'No. Well, there's a lovely little dark-skinned princess. But she's just been out with Manfred in the Bermudas. You know what he's like. She'll be completely exhausted. Other than her there's a couple of English blondes. You can guess that Astrid will be after them.'

'Well, I'd better take her in,' Laurie said.

'Pity,' Angus said wistfully. 'I could have made wonderful music with her.'

'Don't worry, I'm sure Whittaker will find you someone to play with.'

'I wouldn't mind one of the boys, but he's not into men.'

Laurie took Andrea's forearm and led her down the long hallway. With the chain making it impossible to straighten her arms her muscles were already beginning to cramp, and the thin metal loops around her thumbs still bit into her flesh. Andrea still had no idea why she'd been brought to this house or what was going on, but from the conversation with Angus it was obvious that this was a regular event with the girls provided by other masters in *The System*.

There was a large door at the end of the corridor, which Laurie opened. The room beyond was dark, its walls and ceilings decorated in a deep burgundy that matched the carpet. Upon one wall was a large rectangular mirror with an elaborate gilt frame.

Laurie guided Andrea inside and closed the door behind them. As Andrea's eyes became accustomed to the light she saw five other girls. Like her they were dressed in bizarre costumes that lewdly exposed their bodies. They were all gathered around a large oval bed in the middle of the room, its mattress upholstered in burgundy velvet.

There was no mistaking the 'dark-skinned princess' Angus had referred to. She was a tiny girl with long black hair that reached down almost to her buttocks, an olive complexion and eyes so dark they were almost black. She was wearing a tight and very short red rubber tube dress, its strapless bodice taut across her jutting breasts. The hem of the dress barely covered her buttocks.

The two English blondes were there too, both identically dressed in black PVC catsuits and patent leather ankle boots with stiletto heels. The catsuits had cut-outs so their breasts were exposed, and between their legs, so that their sexes and almost half of their buttocks were uncovered.

Of the other two girls one was a redhead, her hair cut short, her body clad in a red velvet waspie that left her breasts bare. The corset was cinched tightly around her waist, its boned material cutting deeply into her flesh, the laces at the front dangling down over her belly, her mons shaved and hairless. She was wearing skin-tight red leather thigh boots.

The last girl had had her head shaved and oiled. She was wearing a white rubber girdle, its short suspenders hooked into white rubber stockings. The bra of the girdle had been folded down under the girl's very full breasts, pushing them up. She had cherry-like nipples, both of which had been pierced, a thick gold ring inserted into the puckered flesh. A gold chain was clipped to these rings and attached to the middle of it was another which ran vertically down. It, in turn, was attached to two rings that had been inserted in each side of her shaven and hairless labia. Andrea could see, emerging from the top of the white rubber stockings, a tattoo of a red and blue snake, its coils wrapped around the girl's thigh. The head of the snake, its mouth open and its fangs extended, was immediately under her sex, the reptile's eyes staring right up into it.

Laurie led Andrea over to the bed.

'Let's see now,' she said, looking from one girl to the other. 'Yes, that would make an interesting combination.'

She took out the small key that unlocked the thumb-cuffs and opened one of them, allowing the chain around Andrea's neck to be pulled clear. Then she took the open cuff and clipped it to the brunette's left thumb. It was only then that Andrea noticed that all the girl's were bound together in some way. The brunette's right wrist was strapped into a leather cuff that was clipped to a cuff on one of the blonde's left ankle. Her right ankle, in turn, was bound by metal cuffs to the tattooed girl's left wrist. The other blonde's right hand was locked to the vertical chain that ran between the nipple and labia rings.

To complete the daisy chain, Laurie went to a small chest of drawers and took out another set of leather cuffs. She wound these around Andrea's free hand and pulled her arm back so she could strap the other cuff around the redhead's ankle. She snapped little brass padlocks over the buckles on the cuffs so prying fingers had no chance of taking them off.

Without another word Laurie turned and left the room. Andrea heard the key turning in the lock.

'She's new,' the tattooed girl said. With a rattle of chain she stretched forward and ran her hand over Andrea's chest, her fingers digging into her breasts. 'Not pierced, though.' She pinched Andrea's nipples as if testing how they would react to a piercing gun.

'She's the last,' one of the blonde's said. 'I'm Penny.' She nodded to the brunette. 'That's Georgina.'

'I'm Tanya and she's Kim,' the redhead said, indicating the one with the body piercings.

'And I'm April,' the other blonde said.

Andrea smiled uncertainly and introduced herself. 'Are we allowed to talk?' she asked.

'In here we can do anything, sweetheart,' April said. 'Now can we get on with it?' She turned to the redhead and kissed her lightly on the lips. 'Jesus, Tanya, I'm so turned on already.'

'We all are, sweetie, otherwise we wouldn't be here, now would we?' The redhead reached across to the blonde and kissed her breasts. She tried to raise a hand to touch her body but it was cuffed to the other blonde's wrist and she couldn't do it. Instead she managed to squirm her breasts against Tanya's.

'What are we supposed to do?' Andrea asked,

feeling confused by the whole episode.

The tattooed woman laughed. 'We're supposed to get it on.' She slipped a hand down to Andrea's thighs, then pushed up under her dress. 'Like this.' Andrea felt her fingers prodding against her sex, easing the thin gusset of the black satin panties aside.

'No,' she murmured, not wanting to upset anyone, but not sure that she wanted to acquiesce either.

'Oh yes,' the tattooed woman insisted. She nodded to the redhead and the brunette. The redhead immediately stretched out her leg, pulling Andrea's hand that was cuffed to her ankle across the bed. The brunette pulled her arm outwards so that Andrea's other hand was pinioned up above her head. She tried to close her legs but other hands grabbed her ankles and pulled them apart as Kim's hand snaked between her thighs and determined fingers probed the mouth of her vagina.

Andrea felt a wave of panic. The long zip at the front of the dress was pulled down and the dress peeled back. She felt hands and mouths descending on her body. Her bra was pulled up over her breasts and a mouth smothered each nipple, teeth biting and pinching at her puckered flesh. The tiny panties were literally ripped. With her legs stretched apart more fingers joined Kim's crude exploration of her sex. A finger circled her clitoris while others prodded and probed her vagina and her anus.

'No...' she complained, struggling to get up.

'Yes,' Kim hissed in her ear. Her tongue wormed over Andrea's lips and then she kissed her aggressively, thrusting her tongue in her mouth and mashing their lips together.

Andrea tried to twist away but five pairs of hands held her firm, pushing her down onto the velvet upholstery. She felt a face dipping between her legs, soft wet lips sucking on the flesh above her lacy black stocking tops. A tongue slithered rapidly up towards her labia, licking at the fingers that already played there until they moved aside, leaving the tongue free to explore intimately.

As it delved into her vagina Andrea felt a huge rush of secret delight. Though the fingers had allowed the tongue freedom to explore, they still mauled at her clit and between her buttocks. Andrea had never felt anything like it. Her panic gave way to excitement, waves of arousal flowing over her. With the mouths still sucking her breasts and nipples it seemed there wasn't a single erogenous zone in her body that wasn't being cruelly stimulated, and the impact from them all was simply overwhelming.

She raised her head and looked with misty eyes at the five bodies enveloping her, their hands and mouths concentrating on delivering pleasure. Tanya knelt immediately above her and was looking down into her eyes. The redhead leant forward and kissed her on the mouth, thrusting her tongue between her lips just as Kim had done. It was hot and wet and Andrea's joined it in a lascivious dance.

Andrea was coming. It was not like any orgasm she'd experienced before. She was swamped with joy. There were two fingers deep in her bottom, working expertly, and the tongue in her vagina had been replaced by three equally clever fingers. They rubbed against each other, frotting against the velvety wet walls while the tongue teased the sensitive rubbery nub of her clitoris. Not to mention the mouths that sucked hungrily at her nipples, occasionally pinching them with their teeth, and the hands that kneaded the pliant flesh. All these feelings came together, mounting like a wave about to crash down on the shore. And of course, overlaying it all, was the thrill of her powerlessness, the fact that she was pinioned to the bed and unable to move, her bondage on this occasion provided by the hands that held her down.

She shook her head, wanting to free herself from Tanya's kiss, then arched back until the sinews of her throat corded like rope. Suddenly all the feelings in her body, all the hands and mouths that pawed and sucked at her flesh, centred themselves on her clitoris. She let out a long low scream as her whole body quivered, her orgasm so intense it was as if a red-hot needle had pierced the most sensitive part of her. The sensation was painful - but it was pain, like the sting of the whip, to be gloried in.

The other girls allowed her climax to take its course, their hands slowly leaving her body. She gasped as the fingers left her anus and her sex contracted sharply as her vagina was vacated, renewing all the tremors and trills of orgasm, her clit and labia throbbing vigorously. She felt the tensions in her arms slacken as Tanya and Georgina moved their limbs, allowing her wrists more freedom.

Now the focus of the mass of bodies changed and the girl with the body piercing found herself to be the centre of attention, hands smoothing over the white rubber girdle she wore, lips sucking at her breasts. The girl's legs were drawn apart and Andrea twisted around until she found herself staring at her sex, the two gold rings that pierced her labia just under the fourchette joined together by a clip that was attached to the end of the chain. Her sex was hairless and glistening like it had been oiled. The mouth of her vagina winked open, the scarlet interior dripping a sticky sap onto the fangs of the red and blue snake that decorated her thigh.

A hand was pushing Andrea forward and she made no effort to resist. She felt the cool PVC of Penny's catsuit against her back as the blonde positioned her between Kim's legs, helped necessarily by the other blonde since their hands were cuffed together. Not that Andrea needed any encouragement. Her orgasm and the incredible feelings the girls had generated in her body had left her hungry for more. As she dipped her head between Kim's thighs, inhaling the unique aroma of rubber, the girl arched her buttocks up off the bed, angling her sex towards Andrea. Andrea kissed it. She prodded her tongue into the slit of wet flesh and moved it to her clit. But with the rings that pierced the upper section of her labia clipped together Kim's clit was still partly hidden and Andrea had to wriggle the tip of her tongue under the little hood of flesh before she could feel the swollen button of nerves. The restriction appeared to make no difference to the girl, however, and she gasped loudly as Andrea's tongue butted against her clit.

Andrea felt something tugging at her wrist, pulling her arm up over Kim's body. Without breaking the rhythm of her tongue, Andrea glanced up to see that Tanya was kneeling astride the girl's shoulders, her ankle still chained to Andrea's wrist. Immediately Kim raised her head to plant her mouth firmly on Tanya's sex. She licked it with long strokes of her tongue, then moved her mouth down to Tanya's thighs, sucking on the corded sinews above the tops of the leather thigh boots.

Once again all the girls began to join in. Penny and April crawled along the bed until they could reach Tanya's body.

Penny picked up the chain from the nipple rings and

stretched it taut, pulling Kim's breasts up and stretching the puckered flesh of her nipples against the fat gold rings until it looked as if they might be torn free. But though the pain from this treatment must have been extreme it only served to fuel the fire that was obviously consuming Kim, and Andrea felt her sex pulsing wildly.

April, in the meantime, had used a single finger to probe down between Tanya's legs, stroking the redhead in a competition with the tip of Kim's tongue. When the finger was covered in saliva she pushed it lower and penetrated the girl's anus, screwing her single digit inward until it was buried to the knuckle.

Andrea concentrated on what she was doing, but she felt hands smoothing over her back under the open dress and down over her buttocks. She thought she felt Georgina's long black hair sweeping against her flesh as the brunette squeezed one of her breasts, crushing the erect nipple. Her other hand, bound to Andrea's by means of the thumb cuffs, pulled Andrea's arm behind her back until she could reach Andrea's swollen labia. Though she had only just come her body reacted to this new intrusion with a wild throb of delight.

Kim was coming. Andrea could feel her trembling. She was bound to the bed by the weight of hands and bodies that held her down and this, as it had with Andrea, only seemed to increase her excitement. She arched off the bed and came, muffling her scream of delight by pressing her mouth hard against Tanya's open sex.

As Andrea felt Kim's sex contracting powerfully she saw April reach down to the floor at the side of the oval bed. She lifted up a pink rubber dildo. The dildo was about two feet long and shaped at both ends to resemble a male phallus. Without any hesitation April fed one end of it into her sex. Then she turned and rolled onto her back, pulling Penny, perforce, with her. Penny immediately grabbed the protruding end of the dildo and swung herself astride the blonde, the PVC of the catsuit creaking. She positioned the bulbous end of the dildo at the mouth of her vagina then sunk down on it until the whole pink tube had disappeared and her labia was crushed against April's pubic hair. Both girls began to rock against each other, grinding from side to side and gasping loudly as their clits were crushed exquisitely.

Andrea raised her head from Kim's sex, her chin and cheeks glistening with the girl's juices, and rocked back on her haunches, her knees spread apart. She licked her lips, tasting the delicious sweetness of the girl's spending, but as she did Tanya leant forward, hooked her hand behind her neck and kissed her full on the lips, her tongue plunging deep into her mouth.

As this new assault generated waves of intense delight, Andrea felt something cold and hard prodding between her labia. She wrested her mouth away from the redhead and looked down between her legs to see Georgina pushing another smooth dildo up into her pussy. It encountered no resistance and Andrea felt the torpedo shaped tip drive right up to the neck of her womb.

Georgina pulled it out again, almost to the mouth of her vagina, then pumped it back until it nearly disappeared.

Andrea moaned. She looked across the room at the large gilded mirror. She could see the reflection of the six girls, their bodies banded by tight costumes, flesh swamping flesh. This was not, she realised with a shock, a spontaneous exhibition of passion. It had all been carefully arranged. Behind what she was sure was a two-way mirror the guests she had glimpsed sipping champagne had been assembled to watch. Or perhaps there was a television camera relaying all to monitors in the front room so they could observe events from there. Whatever the technical details, they had been brought into this room to perform for the assembled guests.

A hand was pulling her over onto her side. She fell against Penny's thigh, the black PVC feeling strange against her cheek. More hands were turning her over onto her back and pulling her legs apart, the dildo still jammed between her thighs. She watched Tanya straddling her shoulders, her red waspie girdle cinched tightly around her waist, her labia, framed neatly at the top of the red leather thigh boots, as smooth and hairless as Kim's had been.

Tanya lowered her sex to Andrea's mouth and she licked it eagerly, the dildo Georgina was ploughing into her vagina with ever increasing enthusiasm provoking a whole new range of sensations. The breadth of the phallus as it was driven home stretched her labia apart, pulling her clitoris like an elastic band. In no more than four or five thrusts, with Tanya's hot wet sex leaking over her face, Andrea was coming again. Everything she saw, everything she smelt or heard or felt, only added to the extraordinary arousal that was racing through her body. She could see Penny and April out of the corner of her eye, their bodies rocking as they clung to each other, the double dildo buried inside them, their breasts moulding together. The aroma was incredible too; the scent of musky and expensive perfume mixed with the much more primitive aroma of sex. And then there was the little gasps and moans and noises, each with its own register of desire and need, each voice different and distinct, each provoking Andrea further.

The dildo was pulled almost out of her sex, then plunged back in again. As she felt her flesh parting to admit it her orgasm broke over the unyielding plastic, her clitoris pulsing violently. At exactly that moment Tanya came too, grinding her sex down against Andrea's mouth, spreading her labia apart so the little knot of her clit was trapped against Andrea's chin. The two women quivered, the orgasm in one feeding the other, increasing the power of both.

But it was not over. Hands pulled at Tanya's body. While Penny came up behind her determined to fuck her with the double dildo, Georgina planted her sex squarely on April's face, handing the dildo to Andrea, its surface glistening with her juices. As she settled on April's mouth, and April used her tongue on her clit, she took Andrea's hand and directed the dildo down between her legs. And so it went on, an endless round of endless sex; mouths, lips, tongues, fingers, penetrating, probing, frotting the nearest breast or nipple or anus or cunt, waves of delicious sensation egging them on and on.

Chapter 4

'So what happens now?' Andrea asked.

Half an hour before the six girls had been taken from the room and stripped of their scanty clothes. They had been taken to a large bathroom upstairs where they were showered. They were ordered to remove all their make-up, including their nail varnish, and were then led into an adjoining bedroom, naked, the towels they had used to dry themselves taken away.

'We wait,' Tanya said.

'And keep quiet,' April put in. 'We're not supposed to talk now.'

'We'll be punished if they hear us,' Penny added.

'But what happens next?' Andrea insisted, her curiosity getting the better of her.

None of the girls answered.

'You'll be collected and taken away,' Kim whispered.

'Taken away where?'

Kim shrugged.

Almost immediately the door opened and a tall woman, seemingly in her early fifties, strode in. Without a word she grabbed Tanya's arms and pulled them behind her back, clipping her wrists together in metal handcuffs. She dropped a pair of high heel shoes on the floor and waited while Tanya climbed into them. Tanya glanced back at Andrea with an uncertain smile, as she was frog-marched out of the room.

Only a few minutes later the door opened again and the ebullient man Laurie had talked with earlier in the hall entered. He glanced at all the naked women appreciatively, then decided upon Kim, pulling her arms behind her back and cuffing her wrists in metal cuffs. He placed blue high heels on the floor and led her away the moment she had put them on.

In the next ten minutes April and Georgina were collected by various women, both given nothing to wear but stilettoed shoes, and both bound with their hands behind their backs in metal handcuffs.

The next time the door opened it was Laurie. She

moved to Andrea and handcuffed her arms behind her back. White shoes were put in front of her and as soon as Andrea had wriggled feet into them Laurie took her arm and led her out, leaving Penny alone.

They walked downstairs, Andrea's unsupported breasts quivering with each step. The house was eerily quiet. Once on the ground floor they headed to the sitting room. To Andrea's astonishment Charles Hawksworth was standing by the large stone fireplace, a glass of champagne in one hand.

'Good evening,' he said. He looked at her intently with those cold blue eyes, and Andrea felt her heart stand still. 'I needed to come and explain to you what is happening,' he said.

'Thank you, master,' she replied sincerely.

'You've been auctioned off to the highest bidder in *The System*. Various masters send their representatives to watch these little...' he searched for the right word '...performances. And of course, the tape you made on the plane has been circulated too.'

'Yes, master.' Clearly her training at Marie-Claire's hands had been effective. Though there was no doubt in her mind that she would have preferred to stay with Charles, she felt a sharp stab of excitement at the thought of being taken to a new master. Her mind began to run riot as she imagined what he would be like.

'But you have to choose. You must agree to go. You must agree to comply with what I have planned for you. Do you understand that?'

'Yes... master.'

There was a choice, of course, but it wasn't a viable one. If she refused to go she would be sent home, back to her normal humdrum life. She would never see her master again, or be part of *The System*. And she definitely wasn't ready for that yet. She had come this far on her journey of exploration, and she certainly didn't intend to turn back now.

'So will you do as I demand?'

'I'll do whatever you want of me, master,' Andrea said in a clear calm voice.

'Good.' He nodded and a smile flickered in his crystal eyes. 'You must obey your new master as you would obey me. If you do not you will be punished. If you refuse punishment you will be sent home. And that will make me very angry.' The ghost of a smile was gone and his eyes now burned into her with a new intensity.

'I won't let you down, master, I promise,' Andrea said determinedly.

'The car is waiting,' Laurie put in.

'Leave us for a moment, will you?' he said, without looking at her.

With just a tiny hint of disapproval Laurie walked to the door and closed it behind her.

'I'm not really supposed to be here,' he confided, once they were alone. 'I came because you're very special, Andrea. I shall miss you.' He walked to her, his eyes examining her naked body. She realised in the whole time she had been with him he'd rarely seen her completely naked; usually he had her dressed in lingerie or other outre garments. He raised his free hand and touched a finger against her nipple, watching as it stiffened. Then he moved around behind her and she felt a hand smoothing against her buttocks, the marks from Marie-Claire's cane at last entirely faded away. His finger dipped down between her legs and she thought she heard him give a little sigh as it slid between her warm damp pussy lips. 'You're wet,' he whispered.

'Yes, master.' Her sex trembled at the rare contact, flexing against his digit. Almost unconsciously she pushed her buttocks back against his thighs. His finger slid nearer to the mouth of her vagina.

'There are many things I haven't done with you yet,' he said. She thought she could feel his cock growing and surreptitiously ground her buttocks against it.

For a moment he pulled away, walking back to the fireplace and sipping his champagne, as if trying to make his mind up about something, though his eyes didn't leave her body for a moment. There was a bulge pushing out against the front of his trousers. Then he put the glass on the mantelpiece, seemingly having made a decision.

'Come here,' he said, pointing to the carpet in front of him.

Andrea felt her pulse racing.

'Kneel.'

Andrea obediently sank to her knees. She found herself staring at the tented material just inches from her spellbound face.

Charles unzipped his immaculate trousers and eased his vibrant erection from its nest of underwear and shirttails. Without waiting for orders Andrea leant forward and sucked the sword of flesh into her mouth until his glans was buried against the ribbing at the back of her throat and her lips and nose were nestled in his pubic hair.

Charles caressed her long blonde hair. He laced his fingers into it then pulled her head back, until the ridge of his glans was pursed at her lips. She ran her tongue over it, knowing how sensitive he was there, and he moaned, his body trembling.

'I shouldn't be doing this,' he said, almost to

himself. But he held her head tightly and pushed deep into her mouth again.

Andrea used her tongue on the thick tube of his urethra. She wished she had the use of her hands to cup his scrotum, jiggle his testes and penetrate his anus, but she was going to have to do everything with her mouth. She wanted him to come in her mouth. She wanted that desperately. Pulling her head back she allowed him to slip from her altogether, then used her lips and teeth to gnaw delicately down the length of his shaft, pushing it back up against his shirt front. She felt the veins in his phallus throbbing.

'No,' he said quietly, but made no attempt to stop her.

Having reached the base of his shaft she slowly and sensually worked her way back. When she reached the glans she eased it into her mouth, bathing the smooth pink flesh with saliva and running her tongue over it.

Then she repeated the process, but this time instead of moving up the shaft again, she dipped her head lower and managed to suck his balls into her mouth, one by one. Once they were both captured she sucked on them gently, moving her tongue between them. She heard him groan quietly and felt his cock jerk as a result.

'No,' Charles moaned softly.

Letting his balls slip from her she pulled back and sank her mouth back over his pulsing helmet, her lips a tight seal around it. She felt it swell even further and knew he was going to come. His hands were no longer holding her head, though his fingers were still entwined in her hair, stroking limply as he concentrated on his own pleasure.

Andrea felt his glans lurch and he erupted into her throat. As she swallowed desperately a second violent discharge was clearly imminent, but Charles pulled out, gripping his cock in one fist while the other in her hair pulled her head back and held her face upturned, and he ejaculated over her closed eyes and open lips.

Eventually it was over. Charles rocked back on his heels, gasping, his shoulders sagging from the ferocity of his release. As though a little dazed he pulled a handkerchief from a pocket and wiped his dwindling penis.

'I shouldn't have allowed you to do that,' he said seriously, a tone of reproach in his voice.

But nothing could dissipate the euphoria Andrea was feeling. Against all the odds, and his wishes, she had made her master come. That would give him something to remember her by. She looked up at him, her eyes sparkling with mischief. Whatever the next six months brought she would have this memory to cherish.

'You have to go now,' he said, and used the handkerchief to dab her face; an action Andrea happily perceived as unguarded affection. He went to the door and opened it. Laurie was waiting outside, and gave him a disapproving look.

'You can take her away now,' he said, and then walked out of the room without looking back.

There was a large white van waiting outside the front door. Its back doors were open and Andrea saw there were two slatted wooden bench seats on either side of the interior. A large woman in a white nylon overall, thick white tights and white plimsolls, was sitting on one of the benches. She had jet-black hair that was pulled back into a tight bun. The buttons of the overall were stretched tightly over her ample bosom, strained almost to bursting point.

'Why is so late?' she said in fractured English as Laurie presented Andrea to her.

'I'm sorry,' Laurie said.

'Is not good to keep me waiting,' the woman said, her accent distinctly Spanish. 'I not like.' She took hold of Andrea's arm and pulled her up into the van, then guided her down onto the bench. Andrea noticed two padded black leather cuffs were secured to the slats on either side of her. 'Keys,' the large woman said.

Laurie handed her the keys to the handcuffs. The woman twisted Andrea around then unlocked the cuffs. She handed them back to Laurie. Quickly the woman pulled Andrea's wrists into the cuffs on the bench, buckling them tight so she was unable to get up.

'We go now,' she said. Without another word she swung the van door shut in Laurie's face and pounded on the side panel twice. Immediately the engine started and the van drove off, the tyres spitting gravel as they tried to get a grip.

The back of the van was completely separated from the driver, and with no windows it was only lit by a single overhead light.

'My name is Maria,' the woman said. She sat on the bench opposite Andrea. 'You know you must do what I say?'

Andrea nodded. She wanted to ask where they were going, but as the woman already appeared to be annoyed with her she decided not to risk increasing her wrath.

Maria stared at her naked body, avidly watching the way the movement of the van made her breasts sway. Andrea's nipples were still puckered and she could feel her sex lips were wet. The experience with her master had left her almost breathless with pent-up desire.

After a few minutes the lumbering woman moved and sat next to Andrea, her meaty thigh crushing against Andrea's bound wrist. She raised a hand and cupped Andrea's left breast, almost tenderly.

'Is nice,' she said. 'We get on well, I think.'

There was a leather suitcase on the floor at the side of the bench, and Maria picked it up and opened it. She took out a black leather helmet, obviously intended to enclose the head completely, and got unsteadily to her feet, pulling the helmet over Andrea's head. The woman carefully threaded Andrea's long hair through the lacing at the back, so it formed a ponytail, then tugged the garment down over her face. She made Andrea bend forward then began tightening the lacing until the soft leather was stretched over her contours like a second skin. There were oval holes for her eyes and her mouth, but they were fitted with metal zips so they could be closed easily. The only other openings were at her nostrils.

Maria worked her fingers over the leather, smoothing out the last wrinkles, then tightening the laces one last time before tying them off at the nape of the neck. Then she took a small oval rubber ball from the case.

'Open mouth,' she ordered.

Andrea obeyed, somewhat reluctantly. The rubber was pushed between her lips and sealed in place by closing the zip in the leather helmet. It pushed Andrea's tongue down, making it impossible for her to talk.

Maria took a black catsuit from the case, the aroma of leather filling the van. She knelt in front of Andrea and began by inserting her feet into the legs of the garment, tugging it up to her waist. The legs were tight and it took a great deal of effort but Maria was strong and manhandled Andrea until the leather smoothly cosseted her legs. Then she undid the cuff at Andrea's right wrist.

'Stand,' Maria ordered gruffly.

Andrea obeyed instantly, though with her left wrist still cuffed to the wooden slats of the bench she couldn't straighten up.

Maria reached into the suitcase again and extracted a small jar of cream and an odd-looking pink rubber pad. It was contoured exactly like a slimline sanitary pad. One surface was smooth while the other was covered with tiny nodules. On this inner surface there were also two knobs, one slightly smaller than the other. Though neither was more than a couple of inches long both were thick and circular. It didn't take a lot of imagination to guess where the pad was designed to fit.

The woman turned her around so she was facing the bench then opened the jar and smeared the two knobs of the pad with cream.

'Open legs wider,' she instructed. 'Push bottom out.'

Andrea spread her legs apart; though she was restricted by the creaking catsuit bunched around her thighs, and angled her buttocks up. She felt the cold objects being pressed between her legs. The creamed knobs slid into her bottom and vagina easily, the breadth of both stretching the tender flesh and making Andrea gasp into the gag.

'Hold in,' Maria said. She took the catsuit and pulled it up over Andrea's buttocks and hips. She smoothed it over her back and over her right shoulder then fitted Andrea's right arm into the leather sleeve.

The catsuit had a long zip running from the cleft of the buttocks, between the legs, over her belly and chest to her throat. Maria zipped it up as far as Andrea's mons, thus holding the rubber pad in place.

'Sit,' came the next curt instruction.

Andrea did as she was told. The woman refastened her right wrist into the leather cuff, then unbuckled the left. She pulled her arm into the vacant sleeve and tugged the tight leather up until it fitted snugly. The woman grasped the tongue of the long zip again and pulled it right up to Andrea's throat, the leather cinching tightly around her slender body, her breasts flattened slightly but still smoothly rounded and shimmering in the dim light.

'Good... is good,' Maria decided thoughtfully, then leant close and zipped up the little oval holes at Andrea's eyes. Andrea was plunged into darkness.

Being deprived of one sense immediately increased the sensitivity of all the others. She became intensely aware of the two protuberances that had been thrust into her body, each jolt of the van's rather harsh suspension pushing them inward. She could feel the little nodules on the pad pressing into her soft labia. They had looked innocuous enough, but now each felt like a little spike. Her nipples, flattened against the tight leather, were tingling too.

All sound was muffled and it was difficult to hear over the vibrations of the engine and the noise from the tyres what Maria was doing, but for the moment she seemed to be sitting quietly.

Until now Andrea hadn't really any time to think. The experience with Charles had left her somewhat stunned, and it was as if she'd been in a dream. Only now was she starting to snap out of it.

She hadn't given any thought to what he'd told her.

She wasn't at all sure what he meant by an auction, or whether real money was involved, but at least now she knew how it was decided which master she should be allotted to. It probably meant he'd already seen her, either that afternoon with the other girls or on the tape Laurie made in the jet, and must have been specifically attracted to her, having to bid more than the others. Presumably Charles knew who he was, but hadn't said anything about him or where she was being taken.

Andrea was determined to make a good impression, as much for her master's sake as her own. She wanted to make him proud of her. She was glad Marie-Claire had trained her so well. She had proved to Charles Hawksworth that she could be a perfect slave, and now she was properly in *The System* for the first time she had another chance to prove herself.

Of course she felt a certain amount of apprehension. With Marie-Claire she had been taught that pain and sexual pleasure were delicately balanced. However hard she'd tried to obey all the orders given, some were simply too difficult to fulfil and she'd been punished on many occasions. Of course she knew that was all part of being a slave. If her master wished to punish her it was easy enough to invent some impossible task she would be unable to complete. That was his privilege. And there was no telling if her new master's regime would be more or less demanding than life with Charles or Marie-Claire.

But punishment was only one side of the coin. Sexual pleasure was the other. It was as though the beatings, the endless hours in cramping bondage or any one of the other torments she'd been exposed to, only increased the sexual tension in her body, like a fire being stoked with wood. The more she was subjected to punishment the more profound her sexual pleasure. That was the equation Charles Hawksworth had first shown her, and though she did not understand why, it was one she had come to realise she could not escape from. Whether it was that she had merely come to associate pain with pleasure, or - as she suspected - there was some mechanism in her body that was able to convert pain into the most intense sexual pleasure, she did not know. But the more she submitted, the more she subjected herself to the whims and caprices of her master, the more she experienced a sexual fulfilment like nothing she had ever felt before, a gratification so profound that she could not bear the thought of being without it. Sex had come to rule her life. She was a slave to it just as much as she was a slave to her master. And for the moment that was simply all she wanted.

Wherever she was being taken the thought of what she might be made to endure filled her with apprehension. But at the same time she was filled with a very real excitement.

The van trundled on, her body rocked from side to side, her wrists straining against the leather cuffs. The catsuit was extremely tight and the leather gusset dug deeply between her thighs, holding the two plugs securely in her body. Not only that, the plugs had spread her labia apart and the little hood that normally veiled her clitoris had been pulled aside so the tiny rubber nodules were chaffing directly against it as she slid about with the movement of the van.

It was over an hour before the van stopped and she heard voices. A hand thumped on the side panel and the van pulled forward again. It did not travel very far. This time when it came to a halt the engine was switched off and she heard the driver's door being opened. A few minutes later the back of the van was opened too and a man spoke in rapid Spanish as he climbed up into the back.

Andrea felt her wrists being released from the leather cuffs and hands pulled her to her feet. She heard the clink of metal and felt something cold being wrapped around her neck. It appeared to be a thick leather collar. It had a long strap hanging down at the back. Immediately her arms were pulled behind her and leather straps were passed around the very top of her arms. They were cinched tightly; pulling her shoulders back and making her stick her chest out. Another set of straps were quickly tied around her arms just above her elbows, and a third around her wrists, each set attached to the vertical strap that ran down her back. Finally she felt soft leather pouches, like mittens, being laced over her hands.

Andrea could smell the man's breath. It reeked of garlic. She sensed him looking at her, then felt his hands roughly handling her breasts, his harsh fingers molesting them through the leather.

Maria said something that sounded like a rebuke and his hands fell away. He leant forward, setting his shoulder against Andrea's waist, and lifted her clean off the floor, one hand clutching her buttocks. As he stepped down from the van Andrea smelt the unmistakable aroma of jet fuel, and heard the roar of a plane taxiing on a runway nearby. They were at an airport!

The man carried her for ten or eleven paces then mounted a short flight of steps. This time she smelt cleaning fluids and leather and the scent of freshly brewed coffee. She had been taken aboard a plane. She was thrust forward and felt herself falling lengthways onto something soft. She was pulled around until she was lying flat on her stomach and then felt two belts, one over her back and the other at her knees, being fastened tightly, holding her down so she could not move.

More words in Spanish. Maria must have got on the plane too, as Andrea heard her voice. The man said his goodbyes, and Andrea heard his footsteps descend the metal steps.

Then everything went quiet. There was a thud that sounded like the outer doors being closed and then a high-pitched whine as the jet engines were started. She assumed Maria was sitting opposite her, but she couldn't be sure.

Andrea struggled to get more comfortable, but without much effect. The straps on her arms had been buckled much too tight. Not only did they bite into her flesh and restrict her circulation but her arms were held so tightly behind her back they forced her chest out so awkwardly it made it difficult to breath, especially as she was face down. As usual her body responded to such tight bondage with little trills of arousal, and she felt her clitoris pulse against the rubber pad. Her vagina was throbbing too, the mouth of it clenching around the plug that stretched it so. This in turn produced a movement in her sphincter, the fluctuations in one communicating directly with the other, the little ring of muscles distended deliciously. The gag, too, was having an erotic effect on her. In the blackness behind the blindfold it was easy to imagine it was a phallus, a throbbing phallus, ready to pump sperm into her mouth just as her master had so recently done.

The plane began to move forward, the hard suspension reflecting every bump in the tarmac. Andrea felt it turn, then the engines began to roar.

Seconds later they were in the air.

As the plane gained its cruising altitude Andrea heard the sharp ping of the seat belt sign being turned off. She thought she heard a footstep moving down the cabin and the chink of a glass, but she couldn't be sure. Enclosed in her cocoon of leather, totally unable to move, Andrea could do nothing but listen to the beat of her heart and savour the waves of arousal that constantly swept over her.

'You must be very uncomfortable.'

The voice came as a shock to her; it was another woman with a Spanish accent, but nowhere near as pronounced as Maria's. Andrea tried to nod her head.

She felt a hand on her thigh. She detected the distinct aroma of champagne. The hand unbuckled the strap that held her legs, then moved to the one around her back.

'Sit up,' the woman said.

Andrea struggled to do so. Bound as she was and with the cramp the bondage had caused it took her a great deal of effort to first roll onto her back, and then to push herself into a sitting position.

'Maria!'

Andrea heard a door at the front of the cabin being opened. The woman said something in rapid fire Spanish. Immediately she felt a hand seize her right ankle. Something was wrapped around it tightly. It felt like a rope. The rope was knotted. The plane banked slightly to the left and Maria's heavy bosom crushed against Andrea as she was tossed to one side. Maria straightened up. Andrea felt another rope being pulled around her left ankle, then a strap like a seatbelt was cinched around her waist, securing her in a sitting position.

The woman said something more. Andrea heard the

crinkle of Maria's nylon overall and an odd mechanical sound. Suddenly she felt her ankles being pulled apart, and at the same time they were hoisted into the air. This had the effect of making her body slide back and her buttocks forward until they were on the edge of the couch. Had it not been for the belt around her waist she would have been pulled off the couch altogether. As it was it held her down, her buttocks poised over the edge.

The mechanical noise stopped. Andrea's legs were pulled apart and held up in mid-air, forming a wide V-shape.

'Very good,' the woman said.

Fingers gripped the zip of the catsuit. Andrea felt the leather springing apart as the tongue was pulled down through her cleavage, over her taut stomach, and finally down between her thighs and right up into the cleft of her bottom. Freed from the constriction and with her legs spread open her vagina and anus clenched and the plugs and the pad that held them in place fell to the floor. The relief was enormous, creating a wave of pleasure that made Andrea's senses reel.

She sensed that the woman was staring at her sex; with her legs splayed apart as they were and tied so securely there was nothing she could do to stop her. She was sure her labia were glistening, the cream from the plugs combining with her own copious secretions to anoint the whole area in sticky wetness.

A hand touched her mons, stroking her sparse pubic hair.

'We will have you shaved,' the woman said, as though to herself. Her finger delved lower. After being rubbed directly against the spiky rubber nodules of the rubber pad for so long, Andrea's clitoris felt raw and she gasped as the finger nudged against it.

'So sensitive,' the woman said. She slid her finger across the little nut of nerves. Andrea felt a huge wave of delight. She hadn't a clue who this woman was, but she obviously had authority. She remembered Charles telling Karen that the masters all had major-domo's to look after their slaves, and she guessed that was this woman's role. And, just like Laurie, she was obviously allowed to indulge herself as she saw fit. Not that Andrea was complaining. After her encounter with Charles everything that had happened in the van had brought her to a near fever pitch of need.

The finger slid down the slit of her labia until it reached the mouth of her vagina. There it dipped inside, a single finger circling the inner flesh, pushing it this way and that but not penetrating deeply. Then it travelled lower and delved into Andrea's anus, doing the same thing, except that the tube of flesh was tighter and clung to her finger more tightly.

Andrea heard the woman move and the finger pulled away. She thought she heard a glass being refilled.

'So what shall we do with you?'

A hand pushed aside the leather catsuit and cupped Andrea's breasts, pulling them towards the opening running down the centre of her body, the two malleable orbs squashed together between the metal jaws of the zip. Each nipple was pinched in turn by sharp fingernails. For some reason Andrea was sure it was Maria who'd done this.

'Take the gag out.'

The zip across her mouth was opened and the rubber gag pulled out. Andrea gasped for air, her saliva dripping over her lips and the chin of the leather helmet.

A finger rubbed her lower lip, playing with the trail of wetness. Then she felt a mouth, warm and wet, closing on hers and a tongue darting between her lips, exploring her mouth very much as the finger had explored her vagina a few seconds before. The mouth was velvety soft and excited her. She inhaled deeply, aware for the first time of the woman's musky perfume. The woman's hands were moulding themselves to her cheeks as her lips played against Andrea's mouth with feathery delicacy.

The woman pulled away, and Andrea was sure she could hear a case being opened. She thought she heard clothes being discarded. There was a little gust of air as a garment of some kind landed on the couch beside her, the material scented with the woman's perfume. Then she thought she heard some sort of harness; metal buckles clinking as they were tugged into place.

The woman again said something in Spanish and Andrea heard footsteps. The door at the front of the cabin closed. They were alone.

A hand touched her left ankle, sliding along her calf and up her thigh. Then two hands were caressing her legs, both moving over her inner thighs, stroking the skin-tight leather. She felt a little draught of warm air fan against her labia. A moment later the same pliant lips that had kissed her mouth were pressing to her sex, moving against her labia with a velvety touch. A tongue pressed into the satiny wet slit, licking up and down before it centred on her clit and stroked it delicately from side to side.

Andrea gasped; if the woman continued she would come in seconds, her sex melting, her juices flowing.

'You want it so bad. This I can see.' The mouth said the words without moving away, the movement of the lips creating a whole new wave of sensations. The tongue tapped lightly on Andrea's clit and it responded with a shock of pleasure so sharp that Andrea gasped and shuddered from head to toe.

'I fuck you now,' the woman purred, the excitement in her voice quite obvious. 'But you not allowed to come. Slaves not allowed to come. You know this, I think.' The voice was suddenly stern.

Something inert nosed into Andrea's vagina. She immediately contracted around it as if trying to suck it in. The dildo was large and broad, and as it was pushed forward, Andrea felt the entrance of her pussy being stretched taut again, the feelings the plug had induced immediately revived. As the dildo plunged deep Andrea felt the supple flesh of her pussy clench and hold it firm. The dildo butted against the neck of her womb. It filled her completely, so completely that for a moment she was overwhelmed by it, her whole body concentrated on the hard rod of plastic that invaded it. There was no escape from the fierce sensations that coursed through her.

She struggled to bring herself back under control. She had a new master. She did not want his first report on her to be of her disobedience. But how she was going to stop herself from climaxing, with every nerve in her body already alight, she simply had no idea. She wrestled against the bonds, hoping the feeling of cramp in her muscles would create a wave of pain that would drown the pleasure. She should have known better. As she tried to wrestle her arms against the leather straps that pinned them to her back, a wave of pain certainly swept over her. But instead of crushing her pleasure it only enhanced it, the feeling of bondage and her powerlessness adding to her excitement as it always did. On the black screen of her mind she saw an image of herself, half sitting half lying on the couch, restrained by the seatbelt, her arms tied tightly behind her back and her legs splayed in the air, held suspended by nylon ropes as the woman knelt at the apex of her thighs, a dildo fastened to her by thick leather straps. The image made her shudder, taking her a step closer to the inevitable.

The woman began to move, pumping the dildo into her. Every time it plunged forward, and the top of the phallus nudged into the neck of Andrea's womb, the woman gasped loudly. She had her hands on Andrea's hips, her fingers like steel claws digging into the soft flesh.

Desperately Andrea tried to hold on. Each forward stroke took her closer to her orgasm, the base of the phallus nudging against her clitoris as the woman thrust. The metal zip of the catsuit was biting into the soft flesh of her breasts. She knew she would never be able to stop herself from coming.

Suddenly she felt the woman's rhythm change, a new urgency making her pound the phallus in and out. Andrea guessed that every time the dildo was pushed forward its base was grinding against the woman's clitoris, and producing a wave of pleasure. She felt the woman's fingers gripping her more tightly. Then, with one final forward thrust, the woman stopped, pressing the dildo up into Andrea and grinding her hips from side to side. She made a strained mewling noise, her whole body rigid.

Only when the noise died away did she relax. Her fingers loosened their grip. But it was too late for Andrea. The woman's final throe of passion had set her off too, the grinding of her hips moving the base of the phallus right across the most sensitive part of her already tenderised clit, her sex clenching around the hard rod of plastic as if trying to milk it. She tensed, trying to hold back, but the image in her mind of her bound and helpless body being fucked by another woman toppled her over the edge and plunged her into a violent orgasm.

When she came round it was like waking from a deep sleep. Her orgasm had been so powerful she could hardly remember where she was, but the bite of the ropes as she struggled to sit up reminded her.

'That was not good,' the woman said. 'Not good at all. You disobey me.'

It was true, of course. There was no point in denying it. The woman could be in no doubt that Andrea had savoured an orgasm. It was a very bad start. She had tried so hard to be a perfect slave but she knew the woman had deliberately provoked her, giving her an order that it was absolutely impossible to obey. It looked as if the regime of her new master was going to be severe.

'You know what that mean, don't you?'

Andrea tried to nod. She knew perfectly well. It meant she would be punished.

Chapter 5

Though they hadn't replaced the plugs when the catsuit was zipped up again, nor the gag, and had taken off the mittens and released the leather straps that pinned her arms, they had clipped metal cuffs around her wrists so her arms were still held in the small of her back. Sitting in a car, with her bodyweight forced back on her arms, made the cuffs cut into her wrists. Thin metal cuffs joined by a short chain had also been clipped around her ankles, the cuffs so tight they too bit into her ankles.

Though Andrea guessed it was late afternoon when the aircraft had landed, it was a great deal hotter than it had been in England and as Andrea had been guided, still blindfolded by the tight leather helmet, into the back of the car, she guessed they had flown south.

As far as she could make out the car was fairly luxurious. The back seat was spacious and the suspension soft, and once they got started there was cooling air conditioning. But they made no attempt to hide her helmet or bondage, so presumably the windows were tinted.

After leaving what was obviously a city the car had started to gain altitude, the road twisting and turning upwards. Andrea's escort barely exchanged a word as they drove on, the sun setting rapidly. The altitude and the lengthening of the day combined to lower the temperature and the air conditioning was switched off, no longer necessary to cool the interior of the car.

At last they stopped and the engine was turned off. Andrea heard the car doors opening and she was pulled out. The balmy evening air was scented with flowers.

'Welcome to *Castillo Adolfi*,' the woman said. 'Take her in, Maria. I go to see Dallas. You can take the blindfold off now.'

The woman's shoes crunched on the gravel. As Maria unzipped the holes in the leather helmet Andrea's eyes adjusted to the faint light and she saw a slender brunette heading towards a huge wooden door set in a corbel arch of the walls of what was a castle. Another woman, a blonde, greeted her with a kiss on both cheeks and the door closed.

'This way,' Maria said.

They were standing in the courtyard in front of the castle with a high brick wall surrounding them on all sides, and a large cast-iron fountain in the middle. The walls were draped with exotic blooms, red and purple bougainvillaea, and white acacia. Maria took Andrea's arm and, walking slowly to accommodate the diminutive steps it was necessary for her prisoner to take, led her to a small door that was set on the other side of the courtyard wall.

The door led to a covered walkway, also dripping with flowers and vegetation. The castle was on top of a hill and there was a spectacular view of the valley stretched out below. In the distance the lights of some large city lit up part of the sky, the brighter lights in its firmament blazing like stars. Andrea saw a plane taking off, its navigation lights blinking.

At the end of the walkway was a long single-storey building that was obviously modern but had been built to resemble the castle, its bricks old and a rose red. Maria unlocked a heavy wooden door and pulled Andrea inside. The building had no windows. Along the right side was a straight corridor that had, on the left, doors equilaterally spaced all the way down its length. Each door had a substantial mortise lock with the key projecting from the keyhole.

Maria opened the fourth door down and pulled Andrea inside. The room was cool with white walls and a polished wooden floor. There was a single bed and a straight chair and a little cubicle at the far end containing a toilet and a shower, the shower made from bright ceramic tiles of a Spanish design. The only bedding was a single white sheet.

'Someone bring you food,' Maria said. 'You sleep then.' She inserted the key into the handcuffs and freed them, then handed Andrea the key to the ankle cuffs. Then she turned and left, the large key turning ominously in the door.

Andrea struggled with the laces of the helmet, finally managing to loosen them enough to drag it off over her head. It was a terrific relief. She pulled the long zip of the catsuit down and struggled out of that too, the leather sticking to her body. Thankfully naked at last, she wallowed beneath the cascading shower.

Ten minutes later the food arrived, and Andrea ate hungrily. It had been a big day. There was salad and salami and bread, all of which Andrea consumed with fervour. Then, too exhausted to do anything else, she lay on the bed, using the single sheet to cover herself, and in seconds had fallen into a deep sleep.

With no windows and no watch Andrea was not sure how long she had slept, but she awoke with a desperate need to pee. With that need satisfied she sat on the bed and looked around the room. At some time during the night someone had come in and removed the catsuit and the helmet and the food tray, as they were no longer lying on the floor where she'd discarded them.

The room was featureless. The walls were plain and the bed bolted to the floor. There were four metal rings set into the wall in a position that was obviously intended to allow a hapless victim to be spread-eagled against it. Short chains were stapled to each leg of the bed with leather cuffs attached to them. In the centre of the room a pulley arrangement hung down from a wooden beam that ran across the ceiling. A rope dangled from the pulley with a pair of heavily padded leather cuffs tied to it. Andrea shuddered as she imagined being strung up by them as she had been so many times with Marie-Claire, her body stretched up on tiptoe waiting to receive punishment.

Perhaps that's what the woman in the car had in mind for her. There was no doubt that she would be punished for her disobedience when her new master was told what had happened on the plane. Of course the woman, whoever she was, had contrived to give her an order she knew full well she would be unable to obey, but in the end, though that made Andrea feel less guilty, it would make no difference to her master's attitude. Obedience was the first requisite whatever the circumstances - she knew that.

Occasionally she heard voices outside in the long corridor and footsteps walking on the wooden floor. As far as she could tell all the voices were female, but she couldn't hear what was being said.

It seemed a long time before any of the footsteps approached her door but eventually she heard the clack of high heels walking along the corridor and coming to a halt outside. The key turned in the lock and a tall voluptuous woman entered. She was blonde, her startlingly bright hair shaped into soft waves that fell to her shoulders, and she was wearing a loose fitting white blouse tucked into a tight and short black skirt.

Her legs were spectacular, long and slender, her thighs contoured by muscle, her neat round bottom pouted by the height of her stilettoed shoes. She had a riding crop tucked under one arm like an army officer.

'This is the *Castillo Adolfi*,' she said pleasantly, her accent a cultured East Coast American. 'My name is Dallas Fox. You will call me Ms Fox. Is that understood?'

'Yes, Ms Fox,' Andrea said. She was sitting on the edge of the bed, and wondered if she should kneel, such was the presence of the woman.

Apparently Dallas read her mind. 'I do not require you to kneel. That is only necessary if the masters require it. I am the major-domo here. I look after all the slaves. And, naturally, they have to look after me.' She smiled a cruel smile. 'Get up, let me have a look at you.'

Andrea got to her feet. Dallas examined her carefully. She took the whip from under her arm and prodded the thick leather loop at the end of the lash against Andrea's mons. 'You will have to be shaved. Completely.'

'Yes, Ms Fox,' Andrea said again. She had expected that, after what the woman had said on the plane.

'Bend over. Spread your legs apart.'

Andrea did as she was told. It was humiliating to expose herself to a perfect stranger in this way, but the peculiar mechanisms of her body turned that shame into a pulsing arousal, her clitoris throbbing strongly as Dallas examined her. The American ran the tip of the whip down between her labia, pushing them apart so her vagina was opened.

'All right, straighten up. You have been to Marie-Claire's, is that right?'

'Yes, Ms Fox.'

'So you know all the rules. Just make sure you obey them. I can assure you that I have a very sadistic streak, and there is nothing I like more than being given one of the slaves for punishment.' She smiled again. 'It is what I live for.'

'Yes, Ms Fox.'

The American stroked Andrea's cheek with the back of her hand. She had long fingernails that had been painted a deep red. She trailed one of them down over Andrea's collarbone and across her left breast, scratching the soft flesh. Then she pinched her nipple with the talon-like nail, leaving crescent shapes in the puckered flesh. 'Nice big nipples,' she said thoughtfully. 'I like that.' She walked back to the door. 'Make sure you obey everything without question, Andrea,' she said sternly.

She opened the door and ushered two girls into the room. They were both short, though one was slim and rather doll-like while the other was distinctly plump. Both wore tight black satin bodies, the legs of the garments cut so high most of their flanks and buttocks were exposed, black leather collars, and ankle strap high heels. The plumper of the two had curly brown hair, while the doll-like girl was blonde. Incongruously they both carried leather attache cases.

'You know what to do,' Dallas said to them. She walked out of the room and locked the door behind her.

'You have to be shaved,' the plump girl said, walking to the shower room. 'Come on,' she said irritably when Andrea did not follow immediately.

'You're English,' Andrea said. 'Where are we?'

'Madrid,' the blonde answered bluntly. 'Now be quiet.' She took a shaving brush, a razor and soap from her case and followed them.

'Lie on the floor,' the plump girl said.

There was just enough room for Andrea to lie down. The floor of the shower room was in coloured ceramic tiles and was cold to the touch, making her already puckered nipples stiffen further. She desperately wanted to talk to the girls, to ask them about the master and life at the castle, but their rebuke had put an end to that. If they reported her to Dallas for talking that would be a second black mark next to her name.

While the plump girl ran water into the washbasin

and lathered the shaving brush, the blonde spread Andrea's legs apart and knelt between them.

'Not much here,' she said, her fingers brushing against Andrea's labia casually. 'Hand me the brush, Carrie.' Carrie gave her the lathered brush and the blonde applied it to Andrea's sex, whipping up a thick cream.

'Raise your left leg,' she said when she had finished.

As Andrea did as she was told, Carrie stood at her side, took hold of her leg and clutched it to her body so it was vertical. The blonde pushed her right leg further over so that her sex was completely vulnerable, then began work with the razor. She started on the thighs, working into the dimples just under her labia, then up onto her mons. Then, stretching and pulling with her fingers she worked over the sex lips themselves, shaving away the fine blonde hairs. They rinsed the lather off once then applied another coat and repeated the whole process.

Andrea's sex was still sore from the previous day and the continual prodding and poking was making it sting. But lying there with two complete strangers doing such intimate things to her was also beginning to arouse her. She was aware of Carrie's breasts pressed against her calf and of the way the blonde's fingers seemed to keep nudging against her clitoris. The black satin body the blonde was wearing had become wet and was clinging to her flesh and outlining her firm bosom.

They rinsed the lather away for a second time, then dabbed her dry with a small white towel. The blonde leant forward, bringing her face to within inches of Andrea's sex, inspecting every inch of the newly shaven flesh for any hairs missed.

'Pretty good job,' she said. 'Hey, look at that.' She pushed her fingers between Andrea's labia and pulled them apart so the mouth of her vagina was open. Andrea knew what she had seen. She could feel a wetness leaking from her sex. 'Better test it properly, don't you think?'

'Don't be an idiot, Dallas could come back at any moment,' Carrie warned, glancing towards the door.

'It's all right. I'll pretend I'm just checking everything's really smooth.'

'What, with your tongue?'

'You worry too much.' The blonde pushed her mouth down against Andrea's sex and licked, from the fourchette to her anus. With one leg still held vertically Andrea's buttocks were partly angled off the floor and her sex was completely exposed, the tongue leaving a hot wet trail that made her shudder. It paused briefly to press against the little crater of her anus, then moved back to her vagina and pushed inside, straining up into the tightness as far as it would go.

'Mmm... she tastes good,' the blonde said, pulling away momentarily. Then her tongue moved to Andrea's clit, circling the little bud then rubbing across it. Andrea moaned.

'Be quiet, idiot,' Carrie hissed, then changed her position. Still holding Andrea's leg she placed her feet on either side of Andrea's shoulders then squatted down over her face, the gusset of the black satin body poised an inch or so above her mouth. Clutching Andrea's thigh with her left hand, pulling it back towards her, her right snaked down between her legs and freed the three poppers that held the gusset of the body in place. Her thighs were round and chubby and the shaven labia that nestled between them were fat and puffy and wet. 'Come on, lick it,' the girl said, lowering her sex until it rested on Andrea's mouth.

'I thought you were worried about Dallas,' the blonde pointed out.

'Don't see why you should have all the fun.'

Andrea pressed her tongue into the rubbery flesh. It was not difficult to find the girl's clit. It was large and swollen and already pushing out from the protection of her labia. Just as Carrie was doing to her, Andrea rubbed the tip of her tongue against it and felt the girl shudder, her ample flesh quivering.

Andrea felt a rush of feeling despite herself. She didn't know the rules at the castle, but she was sure if Dallas came back and found them like this they would all be in trouble. But it was impossible to ignore the sensations her body was generating. Her clitoris felt as tender as it had ever been after the previous day's exertions, but the blonde's tongue was soothing and arousing all at the same time. She could already feel the pulse deep in her sex that was the invariable precursor to orgasm.

'So smooth,' the blonde mumbled, without moving her mouth away.

'Please...' Andrea pleaded, though she wasn't sure what she was pleading for. Did she want them to stop?

'Come on,' Carrie said, squatting lower, pressing her sex down so it was splayed open by Andrea's chin, her clit stretched and vulnerable. 'Harder.'

Andrea flicked at the large clitoris with the tip of her tongue. She heard the girl moan and could see the lips of her vagina throbbing. But her own orgasm was approaching fast. The blonde had pressed her tongue flat against Andrea's clit and was wriggling it and twisting it. It was a fabulous sensation and one that was making every nerve in her body respond. What's more, there seemed to be a direct connection between her mouth and her cunt. The feel of Carrie's sex against her tongue and lips extended and enhanced the feelings in her own cunt, the two somehow joining together. Squirming against the cold tiled floor, with one leg raised in the air, Andrea came, a huge explosion that completely overwhelmed her, every muscle in her body suddenly rigid and locked. Seconds later she felt Carrie come too, the soft flesh melting over her mouth, her copious juices running over her face.

'Well,' the blonde said, straightening up. 'Looks like I'm going to have to do myself.'

She straddled Andrea's right leg just above the knee, freeing the three poppers that held the crotch of the body in place with a single tug. Andrea felt her press down on her thigh. She was hot and wet and gasped loudly as Carrie leant forward, fished inside the black satin body and pinched her nipples one after the other.

'Yes...' the blonde encouraged hoarsely. Carrie pinched her right nipple and pulled her breast out of the satin body altogether. 'God *yes*...' the blonde repeated, her hand strumming rapidly between her legs.

Andrea felt her sex spasm. She shuddered, threw her head back and began to scream. Had it not been for Carrie quickly jamming a hand over her mouth to muffle the sound the whole building would have heard her.

The crisis passed. The three of them sat on the floor together, gathering their composure.

'No one's to know what just happened,' Carrie whispered. 'Do you understand?'

Andrea nodded. It was another act of disobedience,

but this time she didn't care.

They made her up with dark dramatic colours, using eye shadow and blusher. They applied dark mascara to her long eyelashes, plucked and darkened her eyebrows, and painted her finger and toenails a deep red. Her hair was pinned up so her shapely neck was left bare.

Her clothes consisted of a quarter cup bra made from red satin that supported her breasts but did not hide them, a part of matching red satin hot pants and black hold up stockings with broad plain welts. The crotch of the pants had been removed so that her newly shaven sex was clearly visible. Red leather ankle boots with laces down the front and needle-thin high heels completed her outfit.

They made no attempt to talk to her again, their attitude to her returning to the way they had treated her at the beginning, like established pupils at a school who resented the intrusion of a newcomer. They handled her roughly and made no attempt to be pleasant, the intimacy they had shared apparently forgotten. When they had finished Dallas came for them and Andrea was left alone again, the door locked once more.

There was no mirror in the room, but as she glanced down at her breasts swelling from the bra, she could see she looked like a cheap whore. She was sure her make-up was equally obvious.

She sat on the edge of the bed, and felt extremely excited. There was no doubt that she had been shaved, made up and dressed with only one thing in mind: she was going to be presented to her master. Of course that could be in a matter of minutes or a matter of hours. She knew by now that a master was quite capable of having her prepared like this though he hadn't the slightest intention of seeing her that day, or for days to come. It was all part of teaching a slave that their wishes and desires were no longer important. What mattered was the master's whim. It was a reminder that she was utterly dependent upon him.

What made the waiting worse of course was the way she was dressed. The lingerie, designed to display her body so sexily, made her intensely aware of her breasts, her nipples as hard as stone, and her moist sex. If the girls hadn't been so obviously worried about Dallas bursting in on them she might even have thought that they had been instructed to give her an orgasm in order to torment her with anticipation because, far from enervating her, it had set every nerve in her body alight. After the melting softness of a woman's mouth she desperately needed the hard vigour of a man.

Of course there was no telling what her master would do to her; Charles Hawksworth had taught her that. Any expectations she'd had, any idea that he had called her up to his room because of an inordinate desire for her, had frequently been dashed. Even if her new master had chosen her because he had found her particularly attractive, there was no guarantee that he would want to avail himself of her charms. There was also the question of her punishment. The woman who had brought her from England would have doubtless reported her disobedience. There was no telling what frustrations her new master would invent to make sure she remembered her infraction. But that did not stop her hoping that tonight would be different and that her new master would chose to treat her less harshly.

She estimated an hour had passed before she heard

footsteps coming down the corridor again. As the key turned in the lock her heart began to race.

'Very pretty,' Dallas cooed, drifting sexily into the room. She had changed into a red strapless dress made from a glossy material that moulded itself to her body like a second skin. The tight bodice pushed her firm breasts into a deep cleavage while the skirt of the dress outlined her smooth buttocks, shapely hips and cinched waist. The dress was so tight it was perfectly obvious she was not wearing any lingerie, though her legs were sheathed in glossy champagne-coloured tights, their muscles tautened by the height of her red high heels. 'Get up and turn around,' she ordered.

Andrea got to her feet and turned a full circle.

'Yes, you'll do very nicely,' Dallas decided. 'Now come with me.' They walked out into the corridor. The door at the end was open and to Andrea's surprise, as she had lost all track of time, it was dark.

Dallas led her along the flower-draped walkway and into the main courtyard, where the gentle hissing of the fountain was the only noise. The thick wooden door under the corbel brick arch was open and they walked through it into a spectacular vestibule, tiled in terracotta slabs with a circular staircase rising to a landing on the first floor. There was a huge brass chandelier hanging from a chain in the ceiling thirty feet above. The newel post at the bottom of the staircase was hand carved with a griffin wrapped around a heraldic shield, its four panels each etched with a symbolic design.

They mounted the marble steps of the staircase. On the first floor Dallas turned to the left and led the way down a wide corridor, its stone walls hung with tapestries. There was no carpet on the stone flags and their high heels clacked loudly against it. At the end of the corridor was a wooden door set into a lancet arch. To its left an old table stood against the wall, a dome-lidded coffer sitting on top of it.

Dallas opened the coffer and took out a curved oval of thick leather with thin straps extending from each side. Attached to the back of the oval was a black rubber cylinder. 'Open your mouth,' she ordered.

At that moment the idea of a gag horrified Andrea; it would make it impossible for her to intone her master's name as she knelt on the floor in front of him, the mantra of obedience that always affected her so deeply. 'No, please,' she said, trying to show Dallas that it was not necessary.

'Don't give me any trouble,' the American warned. She offered up the gag to Andrea's mouth and she reluctantly accepted it. The black rubber was broad and forced her lips apart. Dallas buckled the straps tightly at the back of her neck.

'Hands out in front of you.' She took a pair of thickly padded but narrow black leather cuffs from out of the coffer and wrapped them around Andrea's wrists. They were joined by a single metal link. 'All right, you're ready now.'

Taking Andrea by the arm, her fingers pinching the flesh with deliberate roughness, the American opened the door and pulled Andrea inside.

The room beyond was lit so dimly that it took a moment for Andrea's eyes to adjust after the brighter light of the corridor. The room was large with very little furniture. There was a long sofa, a leather wing chair, a matching rectangular footstool, and a double bed on the far side. The floor was thickly carpeted. There was a door to the left of the bed and as it was ajar Andrea could see that it led to a white tiled bathroom.

A woman stepped from the shadows. Though Andrea had only glimpsed her briefly in the courtyard the previous day, she recognised her expensive perfume from the aeroplane. The woman had thick long black hair - hair that was as shiny and black as coal. It was combed back severely and gathered into a tight ponytail at the nape of her neck, making her look older than she probably was. She had a long straight nose, arched jet-black eyebrows and eyelashes coated with thick mascara. Her rather hooded eyes were the deepest green, and her complexion was dusky.

She was wearing a lacy black basque, not the structured boned variety that Andrea had been forced to wear at Marie-Claire's, but the modern version, the almost transparent material clinging to her slender frame. The bra of the garment had a plunge front and allowed her breasts to spill out, while the hem flowed into four triangular fingers on her hips, each ending in a long suspender clipped into lace topped black stockings. She wore tiny black briefs in the same transparent material. They clung tightly, following the curve down between her thighs. To complete the outfit she wore a black chiffon wrap, belted at the waist, and her feet were clad in black satin high-heeled slippers.

'Good evening,' she said, walking right up to Andrea, her scent wafting across the room with her.

Andrea was glad of the gag now; it helped hide her disappointment. She glanced towards the bathroom, hopefully expecting her master to appear at any moment.

The woman raised the index finger of her right hand. It was covered with a long conical sheath, like an elongated thimble, made from bright steel. The cone ended in a point as sharp as a needle.

'I hope you are going to be more obedient than the last time I saw you,' she said. She pressed the point of the cone into Andrea's cheek. It was almost sharp enough to pierce the skin. Andrea saw that in fact it was hollow, the point sliced away diagonally. 'I thought Marie-Claire trained her girls better than that. I thought she taught you how to control yourself.'

The finger traced down Andrea's cheek, over her chin and down her throat, leaving a distinct trail. It moved lower, over her collarbone and down to her right breast until it reached her nipple. Andrea shuddered as the point stabbed into the tender puckered bud.

'Are you going to try harder tonight?' She reinforced the point by stabbing the point of the cone into the nipple again.

Andrea nodded briskly, trying to tell the woman with her eyes that she would do everything she could to obey.

'All right, Dallas, get her ready.' The woman turned and walked into the bathroom, closing the door after her.

Dallas pulled her over to a spot in the middle of the room. 'Kneel,' she said.

Andrea got to her knees as the American operated a switch set into the wall. With a whirr of electric motors a rope descended from a hole in the ceiling immediately above her head. It had a large metal hook attached to the end of it.

When the rope had dropped to within a foot of Andrea's head, Dallas took hold of Andrea's wrists and fitted the single metal link between them onto the hook. She went back to the switch again and the rope ascended, pulling Andrea's wrists up. Dallas stopped the mechanism at the point when Andrea was straining and almost lifted up off her knees, her arms stretched above her.

Apparently satisfied with this, Dallas went to one of the chest of drawers that stood on either side of the bed and opened the bottom drawer. She extracted a thick suede strap, walked back to Andrea and wrapped it around her thighs, just above her knees. She fed the strap through the buckle then jerked it tight. Then she manoeuvred the rectangular leather footstool over from the wing chair and placed it in front of Andrea.

'Do you want me to stay?' she said, walking over to the bathroom door and calling through it.

Andrea held her breath. The bathroom door opened. She was going to meet her new master for the first time.

But only the woman emerged. She had stripped off the chiffon robe and her panties, and strapped across her hips now was a thick leather harness, supporting a triangle of black leather that fitted as closely to her belly and the curve of her mons as the panties had done. Sprouting from the centre of this pad of leather was a pink dildo, its shaft moulded to resemble an erect male phallus, a bulbous acorn-shaped glans with a little slit at the tip, and crude extrusions to give the gnarled appearance of protruding veins. Andrea was sure it was exactly like the device the woman had used on the plane.

It was only then that Andrea realised the truth; there was no one else in the bathroom. This woman was her master... her mistress!

'Yes, I'd like you to stay for a while,' the woman responded at last. She wrapped an arm around Dallas' waist and kissed her lightly on the lips. Then she moved to Andrea, the phallus bobbing obscenely as her hips swayed. She stopped when it was a few inches from Andrea's face.

'I think it's time I introduced myself. I am Marchessa Isabella Sanchez. I am the mistress of this castle and, of course, your new mistress. I hope you are not disappointed. From your eagerness on the plane it did not seem that you found female company too... distressing.' She laughed. 'And of course, that brings us to the first topic of conversation this evening. Your punishment. You must learn, Andrea, that my orders are to be obeyed. Other masters, I understand, are more lax in such matters, but I insist on absolute obedience. You are simply not allowed to come without permission. There will be no exceptions. It may please me to provoke you. I will tease you mercilessly but you must not and cannot indulge yourself, unless and until I say that you may. Is that understood?'

Andrea nodded. Her mind was reeling. If Isabella was her new mistress did that mean there were no men at the castle? She remembered how she had yearned for the feel of a man early on. It seemed that desire was definitely not going to be fulfilled.

Isabella circled her slowly. She was still wearing the long steel extension on the tip of her index finger, and trailed it across Andrea's shoulders. 'So, first the punishment,' she said smoothly.

She went over to a large chest on the wall to Andrea's left. There was a leather jewellery box lying on its surface, and Isabella opened it and took out two heavy diamond encrusted pendants that looked like earrings. She brought them over to Andrea and sat on the edge of the footstool right in front of her. The pendants hung from little clips, which Isabella squeezed open. Andrea could see that the jaws were lined with tiny metal teeth.

Isabella leant forward and centred one of the clips over Andrea's incredibly hard nipple. She allowed it to shut and Andrea squealed through the gag, the flesh of her nipple pinched between the little spikes. A wave of pain washed over her, making her quiver. The pain from the second clip, coming hard on the heels of the first, seemed even greater.

Isabella stood up. She brushed a hand under Andrea's breasts, lifting them then letting the firm globes fall back, making the pendants drop heavily and the clips bite even more deeply. 'Would you do the honours, Dallas?' she said.

Andrea saw Dallas smile. It was the cruel smile she had seen before.

'Of course,' she said. The American walked behind Andrea. She heard her picking something up. 'How many?'

'Let's see how we go, shall we?' Isabella said. She gripped the indecent dildo sprouting from her loins and made an almost imperceptible moan, the base of the dildo grinding against her clit.

Andrea saw Dallas position herself at her side. She was holding a whip that looked like a horse's tail, a thousand thin lashes bound into the braided leather handle. It was quite obvious what she was going to do. She raised her arm and brought the whip down on Andrea's left breast. Rather than the single strip of burning pain she had experienced when Marie-Claire whipped her, this felt as if her whole breast was on fire. But it was a stinging sensation that soon turned to something quite different. The pain from the clips had already transformed itself into that unique melange of pleasure-laced pain that turned her sex into liquid, and this new response only deepened it. She moaned into the gag, deliberately shaking her body so the pendants would jiggle and the clips pull at her nipples.

'Look at that,' Isabella said, not missing a thing.

'She loves it.' Dallas stroked the whip down five more times in quick succession, sharing the blows between Andrea's breasts. The tiny lashes reddened the white flesh, leaving little marks like thin scratches. They generated heat too, which seemed to radiate inward, creating sensations that were purely sexual.

Andrea could feel her clit throbbing and a flow of juices leaking onto her thighs. She was glad her legs were strapped together to hide the shameful flood. The lashes of the whip had made her breasts come alive, every inch of them sensitised, the flesh that surrounded the nipples suddenly as sensitive as the nipples themselves.

'Caress them for her,' Isabella directed. 'After pain we should always have pleasure.'

Dallas dropped the whip and knelt behind Andrea, wrapping her arms around her and cupping her breasts. She massaged them with delicious gentleness, her cool hands soothing the superheated flesh. Andrea closed her eyes and rested her head back on Dallas' shoulder, wallowing in the sweet sensations.

'All right, take the gag out,' Isabella said, disappointing Andrea, who was beginning to swoon under the delicious attention.

Dallas got to her feet and unbuckled the strap of the gag, pulling it away. The rubber was glistening with saliva.

'What do you say?' Isabella demanded.

'Th-thank you, mistress,' Andrea stammered weakly.

'Very good. All right, Dallas, you can leave us now.'

'Sure,' Dallas said. Andrea thought she sensed a

note of resentment in her tone. But without another word she left them.

Still holding the dildo in her fist, Isabella stood directly in front of Andrea, the bulbous tip hovering close to her slightly parted lips. 'Suck it,' Isabella said.

Andrea hesitated for a moment, but then leant forward and took the inert object into her mouth.

'Come on,' Isabella said irritably. 'You've sucked plenty of cocks before. Now do it for me.'

Andrea slid forward until the dildo stretched her jaws and its tip pressed into the back of her throat. It felt different to what she expected; softer and more malleable, and when she sucked it the cylindrical phallus seemed to give slightly, almost like a real cock would do.

Isabella moved forward a little, pressing the nipple clips into Andrea's breasts with her palms. Then she took the back of Andrea's head in her left hand and began moving her hips, just as if she were a man pushing his cock in and out of her mouth.

As the phallus forced its way deeper, Andrea could see the black leather triangle being pushed back against Isabella's mons. As it pulled back again the leather lifted away from her belly and Andrea glimpsed the other end of the dildo. It was flared and fitted tightly against her sex. Every time she ground her hips forward the base was stimulating her clit.

It was pretty obvious that Isabella was coming. Her fingers were digging into Andrea's head like talons, and the muscles of her abdomen were rigid. She was breathing heavily too, and making little groaning noises with every forward thrust, bucking her hips faster and faster. She moved her right hand up to her left breast, pulling it out of the bra of the basque. With the finger extension she ran the steel tip right across the soft flesh, then stabbed it into her nipple.

Andrea found that by sucking on the phallus as hard as she could and moving her head she could not only thrust the base of the dildo against Isabella's clit, but move it slightly from side to side. She felt Isabella respond immediately, and this seemed to be the last straw. Isabella thrust forward one last time, jammed Andrea's head against her belly and stood shuddering, her head thrown back, a loud gasp of pure ecstasy escaping her lips. Strangely, though the dildo was completely inanimate, it acted as a conduit for the sensations that coursed through Isabella's sex and Andrea could feel them all. It was like electricity, and affected Andrea almost as much as it was affecting Isabella, her clitoris throbbing wildly, her vagina spasming as if it were looking for something to cling to. With her legs bound so tightly together the feelings were sealed within her sex, and had no way to escape.

For a long moment Isabella stood with her hand hooked around Andrea's neck, holding her head firm, not wanting to move. Then slowly the feelings ebbed away and the tension in her body dissipated. She pulled the dildo from Andrea's mouth, its shaft glistening.

'You're going to be useful to me, I can see that,' Isabella said. She released the link on the padded leather cuffs from the overhead hook. Andrea moaned as she lowered her arms, the muscles cramped for so long registering a sharp protest. She massaged them, trying to relieve the pain.

Isabella pushed the footstool forward so the front edge was touching Andrea's thighs, then bent and unbuckled the strap around them.

'I wish you to lean forward,' she said. 'Rest on the

stool.'

Andrea did as she was told. The leather felt cold against her breasts, still heated by the lashes of the whip and, as she allowed her weight to settle, the nipple clips bit deeply into her hard teats. The flesh had become inured to the pain from them but this brought it all flooding back.

'Good,' Isabella said.

Andrea could not hold her head up for long, the muscles of her neck already strained by such a long period with her arms stretched up, and gradually it sank towards the floor.

Isabella knelt in front of her. She took hold of her left elbow and pulled it over to the front left leg of the stool. Andrea had not noticed before, but attached to the sturdy legs were thin leather straps. The Spanish woman wrapped one around Andrea's arm, just above the elbow. She did the same with Andrea's other arm so that though her wrists were still bound together her elbows were splayed apart.

Andrea watched anxiously as Isabella moved behind her. There were straps secured to the rear legs too, and Isabella buckled them tightly around Andrea's legs, just above the knee, stretching them apart and making it impossible for her to move. For a moment she wondered if she was going to be whipped again. Bent and bound over the stool she was in an ideal position, unable to move with her buttocks perfectly presented.

But Isabella had a far worse torture in mind. She moved around to Andrea's front and kicked off her left slipper, pushing her toes to Andrea's mouth.

'Suck them,' she insisted, thrusting them against her lips. The nails were neatly manicured and painted red. Andrea sucked them into her mouth. Though the nylon looked smooth it felt coarse against her tongue.

She concentrated on the big toe, running her tongue under the sole of the foot as far as it would go. Isabella replaced her left foot with her right. She allowed Andrea to suck on it for a moment then pulled it away. Letting her head drop again Andrea felt the woman move around behind her once more. The moment she knelt Andrea knew what she was going to do. The head of the dildo, still wet, nudged against Andrea's buttocks.

'You are not allowed to come,' Isabella whispered, her voice stern and cold. 'Do you understand?'

Andrea wanted to tell her that was simply impossible; after everything that had happened, after the two girls' teasing mouths and the breast whipping and the nipple clips, let alone what she had experienced moments before as Isabella had come. Just the thought of having the dildo stuffed unceremoniously into her, filling her completely as it had on the plane, made her yearn for it. The reality, the feeling of the dildo penetrating her, would undoubtedly make her come. There was no way she could stop it.

'Mistress, please...' she said quietly. She couldn't think what else to say.

'Do you understand?' Isabella repeated in the same tone.

'I can't, mistress. Please don't expect that of me.'

'If you can't you will be punished.' There was a note of satisfaction in the way she said this. Isabella's hand encircled the dildo, directing it down to the mouth of Andrea's vagina.

'No...' Andrea whimpered, unable to stop herself, as she felt her labia close around the tip of the phallus as if welcoming it with a kiss. Her clitoris pulsed hungrily.

'Oh yes,' Isabella said. She bucked her hips and the dildo sunk into the depths of Andrea's vagina, the flood of wetness making the penetration effortless. The dildo felt huge. It also felt wonderful. It would only be a short journey to orgasm.

Isabella placed her hands on the stool on either side of Andrea and lifted herself, changing the angle of penetration so the dildo was forced downwards. The Marchessa did not pull back. Instead, with her knees still raised off the floor, she ground her hips in a slow, sensuous circle. This produced new spasms of delight.

Desperately trying to fight the growing crescendo of passion that was surging through her body, Andrea tried to concentrate on Isabella. Despite the enormous wave of feeling it produced she deliberately used the well-trained muscles of her vagina to hold the dildo firmly, then thrust her hips up and down so its base would rub against Isabella's clit. Her only hope was to make Isabella come first.

The Spanish woman responded to this with a moan. She dropped onto her knees again and opened her legs a little wider, pushing them against Andréa's. Andrea moved the dildo again, seeing it as an extension of her sex, taking it over. With her vagina clenched firmly she could move it with surprising dexterity. And because Isabella's belly was pressed against her buttocks she could also feel the effect it was having on the woman, every little movement producing a quiver of response.

The trouble was that as she established a rhythm her own orgasm was blossoming rapidly; the other end of the dildo, buried against the neck of her womb, was generating feelings that were just as wonderful. On top of that, the movement was also dragging her breasts from side to side across the stool and making the clips bite into her nipples. This pain twisted itself into waves of intense pleasure, fuelling the fire of orgasm even more.

Oh, she was coming. Every nerve in her body was about to explode. She gritted her teeth and pushed back on the dildo once more. Suddenly Isabella gave a loud gasp, almost a scream. She grabbed Andrea's hips, holding them still, and ground against her buttocks. Her body shuddered then she rocked back until the only thing joining the two women was the dildo. She threw her head back and gave a deep moan of delight, every muscle in her body rigid.

Andrea was coming too. There was nothing she could do to stop herself. But as she felt her inner flesh spasming over the head of the phallus and her clit pulsating wildly, Isabella relented.

'You have my permission,' she breathed through clenched teeth.

Andrea's relief was absolute. Everything that had happened to her that day seemed to be rekindled, combining into one shattering orgasm.

Chapter 6

'And this is Andrea, our latest addition. She was trained by Marie-Claire, and I can assure you it shows,' Isabella announced proudly.

They had dressed Andrea in a gold backless cocktail dress, her breasts without the support of a bra. The dress had a tight skirt and she wore sheer flesh-coloured hosiery and the obligatory high heels, also in gold. Her arms had been bound behind her back by straps around her wrists and elbows, the strap at her elbows pulled so tight they were almost touching.

Isabella was sitting at the table in the intimate dining room she used when she was entertaining on a small scale. Tonight she only had one guest. Margarete Apel was a German. She was tall with a rather long but attractive face, large green eyes and curly auburn hair. Her clothes and accessories all carried designer labels.

'Bring her closer, Dallas,' said Isabella.

The American led Andrea right up to the table. There was a large silver candelabra on the table with four white candles, the flames flickering.

'I had a boy from Marie-Claire myself,' Margarete said. 'He was excellent.'

'Shame on you, and I thought you weren't into men,' Isabella chided.

Margarete laughed. 'Whatever gave you that idea? I like to indulge myself with both sexes. Sometimes at the same time.'

'The only phalluses in this castle are made from rubber or plastic,' Isabella pointed out.

'You do not care for men?'

'No. I prefer to play the role of a man. I do not need one for myself, so unfortunately that is something I cannot arrange for you here.'

'My dear lady, your hospitality has been faultless. I'm sure I can go a couple of days without a cock. I shall enjoy it even more when I get home. I have two particularly fine specimens on my estate. I shall have them waiting for me. Both of them.' She gave a little shudder of anticipation.

'But meantime...' Isabella gestured towards Andrea.

Margarete pulled her chair out from the table and turned it slightly so she was facing Andrea. There was a three-tiered silver stand of petit fours on the table and the German plucked a white chocolate truffle from the top tier and popped it into her mouth. She extended her violet shoe and ran it up Andrea's leg, as far as her knee.

'Not bad,' she said. 'What about the other one?' She glanced over Andrea's shoulder to the other girl Dallas had brought into the room with Andrea.

'That's Berenice,' Isabella told her. 'She's from Los Angeles.'

Berenice was black. She had cropped black hair and skin that was the colour of dark chocolate. Isabella nodded at Dallas, who brought her forward too. She was wearing a tight shimmering silver dress, with a zip that ran all the way down from the mandarin collared neck to the hem of the skirt, and matching silver ankle boots with black laces. Her legs were sheathed in white stockings, and like Andrea her arms were strapped behind her back.

The German eyed her carefully, working her way up from her ankles to her face. 'Have her open the dress,' she said.

Dallas immediately unzipped the front of the girl's dress.

'I had no idea the organisation extended as far as Los Angeles,' Margarete said.

'I don't think it does. Bernie came over to study in Paris. She got involved with Pascal, and he brought her into *The System*.'

Dallas peeled the front of the dress apart. The girl was not wearing a bra or panties. Her breasts were heavy and pear-shaped, and her abdomen flat. A white suspender belt and the white stockings framed the neatly trimmed triangle of pubic hair.

'I should have had her shaved, but she still looks good like this,' Isabella said pensively.

'Mmm... I like that,' Margarete said. 'Come closer.'

Dallas pushed the girl forward. The German raised a foot and pushed it between the girl's calves. She moved it up until the toe of her shoe was touching her sex and wriggled it so that the leather worked its way between the girl's labia. Bernie did not move or utter a sound. 'She's well trained,' Margarete observed approvingly.

'Yes,' Isabella nodded with satisfaction. 'But a little passive. The Borling Sisters trained her. They are too strict, to my mind. They do not allow for any idiosyncrasies. I like to see some real emotion. They produce automatons.'

'Mmm...' Margarete lowered her leg. She got to her feet and stood in front of Bernie, caressing her breasts. With her expensively manicured fingernails, that were varnished a dark blue, she pinched one of Bernie's large nipples. Despite the fact Andrea could see the pinch was vicious, the girl did not react in any way. Margarete cupped her hand under the soft flesh of the breast and pulled it up towards the girl's chin.

'Hold it,' she said, feeding the nipple into Bernie's mouth.

The black girl took her own nipple between her teeth, and as Margarete took her hand away, the weight of her whole breast was suspended by it. Again Bernie showed not the slightest emotion; not pain or pleasure or arousal.

'Remarkable,' Margarete said. She ran her hand down the front of the girl's body. 'Spread your legs apart, girl,' she said.

Bernie obeyed immediately, still holding her nipple between her teeth.

Margarete sat down again. For a moment she stared at the girl's sex. Though her mons was covered with curly black pubes her labia were almost hairless and the mouth of her vagina, which was partially open, was a bright pink in comparison to the dark flesh that surrounded it.

The German picked up a silver salt cellar from the table. It was cylindrical with a domed top. Leaning forward she pushed it up between Bernie's labia into her vagina. She did not utter a sound. Margarete thrust it up until the whole thing had disappeared into the black girl's sex.

Andrea, who had been watching all this avidly, felt herself shudder, glad she was not the one being subjected to the German's attentions.

'Hold it there,' Margarete ordered.

Bernie brought her legs together, squeezing the muscles of her thighs to hold the salt cellar in place. She still made no sound.

'Take her dress off, if you wouldn't mind,' Margarete said to Dallas. Dallas pulled the dress off Bernie's shoulders until it hung from the straps that bound her elbows. The front of her body was entirely naked but for her boots and the white satin suspender belt that supported her stockings, the long suspenders dissecting her thighs.

'Turn around and bend over,' Margarete said.

The girl did as she was told, bending forward, the dress draped over her buttocks.

'Pull that up for me, would you?' Margarete said to Dallas, without taking her eyes from the bending vision before her.

Dallas moved the silver dress out of the way. Bernie kept her thighs pressed tightly together so her labia were pursed between her buttocks, pouting like lips waiting to be kissed. There was no sign of the silver buried in her vagina. Margarete glanced over the debris of dinner that had been left on the table. Her eyes fell on a nutcracker that was poised on a silver platter of nuts. She picked up the metal implement with the faintest glimmer of a smile. 'Closer,' she cooed.

Bernie shuffled backwards until her legs were almost touching Margarete's knees.

'Mmm... very nice,' Isabella said. 'Pretty little pussy, don't you think? This is making me very randy.'

'That's no problem, is it?' Margarete said.

Isabella laughed. 'None at all. Andrea, kneel here in front of me.'

Andrea obeyed at once. Isabella was wearing a long cream silk dress with a plunging V-neck and a split in the skirt that went almost to the top of her thigh. She pulled her chair from the table and turned it just as Margarete had done, spreading her legs apart on either side of Andrea and pulling the skirt to one side to reveal her long, slender legs. She was not wearing panties and her legs were sheathed in tan suspender tights, a band of nylon wrapped around her waist from which two thick suspenders of the same material snaked down at the back and front of her thighs with no sides, crotch or bottom, her sex completely exposed. Her mons was smooth and hairless. Andrea felt a pulse of lust.

'Well, look at that,' Margarete said quietly, her eyes also riveted to Isabella's sex.

'Lick me,' Isabella said to Andrea.

Andrea leant forward and pressed her mouth to Isabella's sex, her tongue forcing its way between her labia to find her clit. At the same time Margarete pressed the top of the nutcracker against the little puckered crater of Bernie's anus. This too, like her vagina, was a delicate shade of pink. But as she pressed forward she met firm resistance. The girl's sphincter resisted resolutely.

'Not very co-operative,' Margarete said with disapproval.

Dallas saw the problem. She went to the table and held up the butter dish.

'Good idea,' Margarete said. She dipped the top of the nutcracker into the butter until it was well coated then thrust it back up against the little hole. This time it slid inward easily, up to the first bulge in the metal arms.

Bernie did not react. She seemed completely unmoved. Margarete glanced over at Isabella, who had laced her fingers into Andrea's hair and was holding her head firmly between her thighs.

'You see what I mean,' Isabella said huskily, the efforts of Andrea's tongue making her breathless.

'No, I like this,' the German said. She pushed the nutcracker deeper, over the first bulge in the metal. Still the girl did not react. 'I think I take her.' She fed the nutcracker right the way into Bernie's bottom. This time the girl made a soft mewling sound and a shudder ran through her body.

'At last,' Isabella said.

'I will take her,' Margarete said, getting to her feet. She moved around the table until she was standing right behind Isabella. She put her hands on Isabella's shoulders and began to massage them, digging her fingers into the flesh. 'I would like to take you too, Marchessa, if that is allowed.'

Isabella looked up at the woman. 'Of course, if you're sure.'

'Quite sure. If you say you like to play at being a man, then I would like you to play at that with me.

And with Berenice, here. That sounds like fun.'

Isabella raised a foot to Andrea's shoulder and pushed her away callously. She got to her feet, turned and kissed Margarete, their lips barely touching, though Andrea could see the tips of their tongues weaving against each other. 'I can be a better man than most men,' she whispered, without moving her mouth away.

'I look forward to it.' The German pulled the nutcrackers from Bernie's bottom. 'Stand up, open your legs,' she ordered.

As she obeyed Margarete pushed a hand between her legs. As the girl's legs were parted the salt cellar slid from her pussy, dropping into Margarete's hand. The silver was smeared with her juices.

'You can release your nipple,' she told her.

The black girl opened her mouth and her breast fell free. There were deep teeth marks in her nipple, and the sudden flow of blood back into the tortured teat made her lose her much vaunted control. She bit her lip and shuddered, shaking her breasts to try and relieve the stinging pain.

Isabella got to her feet and took hold of the girl's tightly bound arms, leading her to the dining room door, with Margarete not far behind. They walked out into the corridor, not bothering to close the door behind them.

Andrea, her mouth and chin coated with the juices from Isabella's sex, felt suddenly bereft. Despite only being called upon to play a minor role in the evening's activities, what she had seen and heard had aroused her deeply.

She was still not sure how she felt about the revelation that her new master was in fact a woman. As she was beginning to understand the *The System* better it didn't altogether surprise her, but she hadn't worked out her own feelings about it. Of course, since Charles had first introduced her to lesbian sex it had been a source of great pleasure to her, but that had only been in the context of serving him. She had learned to love the subtle malleable angles of a woman's body and the tender nuances of their lovemaking. But however many women had possessed her, however many sexual experiences she'd had at their hands, she had always known that sooner rather than later, she would have the virile and animate phallus of Charles or one of his male guests to counterbalance their attentions. In fact, the two experiences had fed off each other, the excitement at one making her overeager to experience the other again.

Now, however, she was faced with six months when it was, she thought, extremely unlikely that she would see let alone be used by a man, especially after what Isabella had just said. There were no men at *Castillo Adolfi*.

The previous night had been wonderful. The frustration of being locked away and neglected was part of the experience of being a slave, and to be given so much attention was a privilege she had not expected. Not only had they been alone - something Charles Hawksworth rarely allowed her - but despite all the tortures Isabella had put her through she had also allowed her to come. And more than that, she had come herself. Whatever Andrea's feelings about the difficulties of living without a man, that counted for a great deal.

Of course, it did not mean her time at the castle was going to be easy. She knew that Isabella was probably just as moody and unpredictable as Charles had been.

Her behaviour last night was probably not at all typical. And what had just happened confirmed that. She had fondly imagined that after wanting her to lick her sex, Isabella might well take her to bed. That hope had been dashed rapidly and she had been left high and dry.

'Up,' Dallas said. The American was wearing a glossy dark red catsuit, clinging to every contour of her slender body. With her arms bound so tightly behind her back it was difficult for Andrea to get to her feet without help, and the American had to haul her up by the shoulders. She looked at her face, then brushed her chin with her fingers, wiping away Isabella's juices. 'Come with me,' she said.

Outside they took the route back to the outbuildings. But instead of returning Andrea to her room, Dallas led her all the way down the long corridor. The door at the end was identical to all the others, with a large mortise lock and key, but as Dallas unlocked it and threw the door open Andrea saw the room beyond was very different. It was much smaller than the others in the block and had no shower area. Its walls were painted a dark blue and it had a thick carpet in the same colour. There was little in the way of furniture. There was a plain wooden framed double bed with a thin mattress covered with a white sheet, and a single chest of drawers to the side of that. Suspended from the ceiling were several chains, ropes and pulleys including a long metal bar right in the middle of the room, attached to either end of which were two thick leather straps. The middle of the straps were wider than the top and had been folded back on themselves to form a thick loop. Underneath these was a wooden stool.

The door was heavily padded on the inside. Dallas

closed and bolted it behind them, then used a switch on the wall to dim the lights.

'Now listen to me very carefully,' she said, pushing Andrea back against the wall. 'You are going to do exactly what I tell you to do, and you are not going to mention anything of what happens here to the Marchessa. Is that absolutely clear?'

'I - I don't understand.' Andrea suddenly felt very uneasy.

'There's no cause for you to understand. Just make sure you do as I tell you.'

'I ... no,' Andrea said determinedly.

'Look sweetie, the Marchessa trusts me. If you tell her I brought you here, I'll tell her you're making it up because I found you with one of the other girls. She's not going to believe you rather than me, now is she? Your life won't be worth living, do you understand?'

'Please, just leave me alone.' Andrea did not want to be drawn into a web of deceit. If Dallas feared that Isabella would find out what she was doing it must be because she'd forbidden it.

Dallas sneered. 'Now that's the last thing I intend to do.' Moving with surprising speed the American crushed herself against Andrea and kissed her full on the mouth, but Andrea resisted, clamping her lips tightly closed.

'Okay, have it your way,' hissed Dallas, breaking away from the clinch. 'Let's give it half an hour, shall we? Then I'll go and interrupt the Marchessa's fun and games and tell her I found you with Carrie.' She smiled, her victorious features mere inches from Andrea's face.

'No...' Andrea felt a chill of fear run up her spine. She knew Charles had once expelled a girl from *The*

System for such a crime.

'No, what? No you don't want me to go to Isabella?'

Andrea lowered her eyes in defeat and did not reply, and this time as Dallas moved forward she opened her lips and allowed the woman's voracious tongue to invade her.

'And don't worry, this room is soundproofed,' Dallas whispered as she moved her lips down Andrea's throat, sucking her flesh. 'No one can hear us. Now go over there and kneel on the stool.'

Andrea saw little choice but to obey. If she refused she was quite sure Dallas would carry out her threat. After only knowing her for a day there was little chance Isabella would believe her, rather than her trusted major-domo. Meekly, therefore, Andrea knelt on the stool. It was just wide enough to accommodate her legs from her ankles to her knees.

'Good girl,' Dallas purred. She went to the chest of drawers and took out a long and extremely broad leather strap. She brought it back to the stool and looped the strap beneath it. 'Now squat right down.' She pushed Andrea's shoulders to indicate what she had in mind, pushing them down until Andrea's head was just above her knees. She then folded the strap up over Andrea's back where her arms were still secured tightly, feeding one end of the strap into the buckle and pulling it tight, forcing Andrea's breasts down against her thighs. She was totally unable to move, her body doubled up and bound to the stool, the wooden surface hard against her knees.

Dallas took a moment to admire her work. She stroked Andrea's hair, then tugged it spitefully, making Andrea wince. 'Sensitive little thing, aren't we?' Dallas taunted.

The dark red catsuit had a long zip running from the neck to the crotch. Dallas took hold of the tongue of the zip and pulled it all the way down, then tugged her arms out of the garment. She was not wearing a bra, and had firm breasts that rode high. Her nipples were already tightly puckered.

Dallas kicked off her shoes and wriggled out of the catsuit. She was wearing tight cream panties that moulded themselves to her curves, thin strings hooking the triangular front to her hips. She took a few minutes adjusting the loops of the leather straps that dangled from the ceiling, re-buckling them until the bottom of the loop hung at the same level as the top of the stool, a few inches in front of Andrea's head. Finally satisfied they were in the right position the American skinned the panties down her long legs. Her pubic hair was fine and blonde. She inserted her legs into the leather loops, her body facing Andrea, so she was sitting in them almost like a swing, then raised her arms and wrapped her hands around the metal bar, pulling herself up slightly so her sex was level with Andrea's mouth. She spread her legs apart, digging her heels under the side of the broad strap around Andrea's back and levering her sex forward by bending her knees.

It was only then that Andrea saw it. As the American flexed a small pink torpedo-shaped dildo nosed its way out of her vagina. It was not much bigger than a large finger. 'Suck it,' Dallas ordered, her voice thick with passion, her labia pressed against Andrea's mouth.

Andrea worked her tongue up to Dallas' clitoris. Like her nipples it was small but hard, and Andrea could feel it pulsing. She rapped her tongue against it, then dragged it from side to side. Dallas moaned. By flexing her legs she could draw Andrea closer or drift away slightly. She allowed the tension to relax enough for Andrea to be able to move her tongue to her vagina. With Dallas' legs spread apart the mouth of her vagina was open, its furry covering slicked back by her own juices.

Andrea plunged her tongue inside. As she did so her own sex throbbed enthusiastically. She had not been given panties to wear under the dress and with her legs doubled up her buttocks were thrust out and her labia exposed to the air. In contrast her clit was trapped under her fourchette, its deep pulsing movements reverberating through her whole sex. Everything she did to the American seemed to affect her as if it were being done to her.

Dallas drew her legs in again, forcing Andrea's face tight between her thighs, her nose butting against her clitoris, her mouth pressed against the entrance to her vagina. She strained her tongue forward, its sinews stretched to the limit as she tried to thrust it deep. As she did she felt Dallas flex her internal muscles and the little dildo was pushed out, nudging against Andrea's tongue.

'Suck on it,' Dallas rasped.

Andrea sucked hard. The dildo slipped into her mouth, Dallas' juices coating it. They tasted sweet. Andrea pursed her mouth around the phallus and pushed it back up into the American's vagina.

'Yesss,' Dallas encouraged. She used her own muscles to suck the dildo deeper. 'Now back to my clit,' she ordered.

Andrea moved her tongue up the slit of her sex. She flicked it against Dallas' clit, then rubbed it across the upper surface. She felt and heard Dallas moan. She rubbed harder, pressing her tongue against the little button of nerves, then wriggling it about. This drove Dallas wild. She gasped loudly. Her legs tensed, forcing Andrea's tongue even harder against her clit, then she made a long low moaning noise. Her whole body went rigid, the muscles in her thighs corded like rope.

Dallas unhooked her heels from the strap and lay back, swaying slightly back and forth, completely relaxed. Andrea saw the little phallus come back into view, slipping out of her vagina and falling to the floor.

Dallas stayed suspended for quite a while, wallowing in the aftermath of her orgasm. Then, with a deliberate effort she roused herself, swinging into a sitting position again and extracting her legs from the loops. 'Now it's your turn,' she said.

She moved away and opened one of the drawers in the chest. She took out a riding crop with a leather loop at the tip, then picked up the same small dildo. 'I see you're in quite a state too,' she said, one hand on Andrea's back, and bent forward thrusting the dildo into Andrea's wet sex. 'Hold it there, or it's double the punishment for you.'

Andrea was responding to her bondage as she always did; the more uncomfortable she was and the more helpless, the greater the sexual charge she seemed to get. On top of that, the taste, sight, smell and feel of Dallas against her mouth had created a huge surge of desire deep within. She was not with her mistress, so perhaps the prohibition against coming without permission did not apply. She desperately hoped not, as she was already on the brink, the effort of keeping the dildo buried deep inside her amplifying the tension in her sex. If she could relax for a moment perhaps her desire would abate a little, but there was no chance of doing that and keeping the slippery little dildo safely in her vagina.

Dallas stood behind her. She raised the whip. It whistled as it came down. *Thwack*! A straight line of pain erupted across her buttocks. Since meeting Charles Hawksworth she'd felt the same sensation many times, but she didn't think she'd ever get used to the effect it produced on her; the searing pain like a thousand needles driven into her flesh and the profound pleasure it turned into - a pleasure like no other. Her sex spasmed and for a moment she forgot the dildo, only reminded at the last moment as it almost slid out. The effort of controlling it produced another wave of passion almost as intense as the effect of the whip.

Thwack! A second stripe burnt across her arse, but this time she was ready for it, with her vagina locked around the dildo. But with so much tension in her buttocks the effect of the whip was far more concentrated and the pain made her gasp loudly, a tear escaping her eye.

Thwack! The third stroke was the hardest. The heat it created seemed to radiate through her, but it was most concentrated in her sex, where it seemed to multiple everything she was already feeling.

Dallas dropped the whip and knelt. She gripped the broad strap over Andrea's back and pulled herself forward until her mouth was flattened against Andrea's melting wet sex. She pushed her nose into her vagina then pulled her mouth lower, centring on Andrea's clit. Her tongue darted out and found the swollen button, flicking it from side to side as she drove three fingers into her vagina. The fingers found the butt end of the dildo and pushed it deeper, so deep it burrowed against the neck of her womb. And that was all it took. All the sexual tension Andrea had felt since seeing the German with the black girl, the way Isabella had used her, and the feel of Dallas coming against her mouth, combined into an incredible crescendo that was suddenly and dramatically released. She shuddered, but the fact that she was so tightly bound made it impossible for her to move and that feeling, that total helplessness, kicked her orgasm to even greater heights. She cried out loud as her sex clenched, closing around Dallas' fingers to produce a final throe of pleasure.

'Put these on and get yourself made up,' Dallas Fox said sternly. 'I'll be back for you in half an hour. And brush your hair out, but leave it down.'

She had brought another small make-up bag with her and dropped it on the bed by the lingerie she had laid out for Andrea. She strode out of the room, locking the door behind her.

Andrea examined the lingerie. Dallas had left an expensive beige silk teddy, its bodice inset with lace, and a thin suspender belt in the same material, the little rubber and metal nubs of its suspenders covered with a diagonal slash of beige satin. There were buff-coloured stockings and the obligatory high heels, in black suede.

Life at the castle had never settled into a routine. The only regular occurrence was that every morning she would help to shave one of the other slave's pubes, just as one of the other slaves would be allotted to shave hers. It was clearly a priority as far as Isabella was concerned that all her slaves, with the obvious exception of Berenice, remained hairless, their labia and mons smooth and sleek. But after the morning ritual the days passed with no pattern.

Like all the other slaves Andrea was given work to do in the grounds, or in the castle itself, but she never knew from day to day what she was going to be doing next. Even meals were served at erratic times. And of course, she never knew when Isabella would call her up to her room or would have guests for whom she, and the other girls, would be paraded and from which the woman would take her choice, just as Margarete Apel had. The only warning she would have of these assignations was the arrival of Dallas Fox with some new outfit for her to wear, as she just had, the dresses or lingerie she brought always incredibly revealing.

Since her first encounter with Isabella three weeks before, the Marchessa had sent for her three times, but never on her own. Another slave was taken to Isabella's bedroom with her, as enthusiastic and dedicated about serving her mistress as Andrea was. On one occasion in an orgy of female flesh, Isabella took great delight in binding the girls back to back and using a strap-on dildo on them, rolling one on top of the other after she'd finished with the first.

Dallas Fox had also taken her to the small dark blue room three times when Isabella had gone into Madrid, each time threatening her with dire consequences if she ever mentioned it to the Marchessa.

There had been at least five guests at the castle since she'd arrived, and Andrea had been chosen by one of them. She was a middle-aged Englishwoman, who'd chosen Andrea and Carrie, the plump girl who had helped shave Andrea on her first day. But she had not wanted them to touch her. Instead she made the two girls perform for her. Andrea was made to whip Carrie's buttocks with a cane, then use a dildo on her. The woman, a statuesque and elegant brunette, sat fully dressed in a businesslike black suit watching the proceedings intently, her hands pressing into her lap. She ordered them into the sixty-nine position and as they sucked and licked at each other's sex Andrea saw the woman's hands slip under her skirt. In seconds, barely moving her fingers, she shuddered, let out a gasp of delight and orgasmed, immediately ordering the girls, who were by now well on their way to their own orgasms, to leave.

The arrival of Dallas Fox tonight was not a surprise. Earlier in the day Andrea had been working in the castle when she saw a large limousine draw up outside in the courtyard and a pretty young blonde in a short peachy-coloured dress get out to be greeted effusively by Isabella. The driver had carried a small case into the castle which indicated, Andrea imagined, the girl was staying the night. No doubt Andrea was going to be one of the slaves who were to be paraded in front of her after dinner.

In the shower cubicle Andrea took out the make-up Dallas had brought. It was much less dark and dramatic than the colours she'd been given to use before, the nail varnish pink rather than dark red, the eye shadow pale and the blusher much less pronounced. The lingerie, too, was much less revealing than some of the outfits she'd been required to put on before.

Andrea got herself ready. After she made up her face she clipped the suspender belt around her waist and rolled on the stockings. They were smooth and silky with broad welts that were pulled into a chevron at the top of her thigh as she clipped them into the taut suspenders. She pulled the teddy over her head and stooped to fasten the three poppers that held its gusset in place. The silk between her legs felt strange. In fact, the teddy was the first time she had been given anything to wear to cover her sex since she'd arrived at the castle.

Stepping into the shoes, which again did not have the precipitously high heels she was usually required to wear, she waited for Dallas to return.

The blonde unlocked the door some thirty minutes later. She inspected Andrea critically. 'All right,' she said. She was holding a leather collar, which she buckled around Andrea's throat. Two metal handcuffs were attached to the front of the collar and she raised Andrea's wrists and snapped them into the cuffs, securing her hands up under her chin.

'Follow me,' she snapped gruffly.

Outside in the corridor two other slaves were waiting. They were dressed identically to Andrea, except that their lingerie was a different colour, one girl wearing a silvery white and the other a pale pink. Their shoes were colour co-ordinated. Like Andrea, their hands were cuffed to a collar.

Dallas led the three girls out of the building. It was a sultry night, and the covered walkway into the castle was redolent with the scent of flowers. The noise of the fountain as they passed into the courtyard was cooling, but the gravel radiated warmth, the stone storing the energy of the hot sun that had shone all day. By the time they walked through the large front door of the castle Andrea could feel beads of perspiration on her forehead. But the interior of the castle was deliciously cool, the sun unable to penetrate the thick stone walls.

They walked to the dining room and Dallas knocked on the door.

'Come in.' It was Isabella's voice.

The three girls walked into the room. Dallas

arranged them in a line with Andrea in the middle.

Isabella and the young blonde Andrea had seen arriving were sitting at the table. Demitasse coffee cups, the three-tiered silver tray of petit fours, and large crystal brandy balloons were arranged on the table in front of them, the blonde's brandy almost gone. She started to giggle the moment the slaves were herded into the room.

'I don't believe this,' she said. 'Is it for real?'

'Perfectly,' Isabella confirmed. 'You're nineteen now, Trissie, and old enough to know the truth. Your uncle had an establishment like mine, in England. Before he died I promised him that I would give you a chance to see what it involved. He wants you to inherit his estate and run it as he did. Naturally, if you're not interested...' Isabella shrugged.

'I'm interested,' the girl beamed. 'I'm very interested. But why didn't he tell me?'

'You were too young. He didn't want to influence you. He wanted you to make up your own mind.'

'So tell me again, these girls volunteer...'

'Perhaps volunteer is the wrong word. There are women who find they need certain things sexually. This satisfies their need. And men too.'

'Men?'

'Certainly. I am only interested in women so I have no male slaves here, but in *The System* there are as many men as women.'

'And they're like these three? I mean, they do everything they're told?'

'Oh yes.' Isabella smiled enigmatically. 'Absolute obedience. That's the rule. If they do not obey they are punished. And if they refuse to be punished they are sent away. But that is rare. The slaves go through a careful selection process and then have to be trained.

Usually that weeds out any that are unsuitable.'

'So if I wanted to, I could have all this on Uncle Henry's estate.'

'Indeed, you could.'

Trissie finished the brandy, then poured herself another glass from the decanter that had been left on the table. 'So what happens now?' she asked, he cheeks glowing.

'Whatever you want. You can take the girls up to your bedroom, or to one of the special rooms we have. It all depends on your...' she searched for the right word, '...proclivities.'

'Mmmm... sounds like fun.' The girl giggled.

'If you'd like me to come with you,' Isabella went on, 'I'd be happy to show you some of the equipment available.'

'No,' Trissie said quickly. 'I think I'd rather work this out for myself, at least the first time. I'm not at all sure what my proclivities are.'

'Good idea.' Isabella nodded approvingly.

'And I only want one of them.' She bounced to her feet. She was wearing a plain black cocktail dress with a box neck and a knee length skirt. 'Her,' she said, coming up to Andrea. 'She's pretty.' She touched Andrea's face tentatively. 'Have her taken up to my bedroom.'

Isabella nodded to Dallas, who immediately took hold of Andrea's arm and pulled her towards the door.

'This really is going to be fun,' Trissie said, sitting down at the table again and finishing her brandy.

Dallas led Andrea up to the first floor and along the galleried landing. She opened a door on the right and ushered Andrea inside.

The bedroom was luxurious. It had a huge double bed, and an antique French walnut wardrobe. The bedside chests were modern, as were the opaque glass lamps on chrome stalks on each of them. The lamps glowed warmly.

'Wait here,' Dallas said. 'And make sure you obey. If you upset Trissie your mistress will be most displeased.' She left without another word.

Andrea stood by the bed, waiting. She wasn't at all sure what to expect. From the conversation in the dining room it appeared that the world of the castle and *The System* were entirely new to Trissie, and how she would react once they were alone together was difficult to judge.

It was about ten minutes before the bedroom door opened and Trissie came in.

'Hi, there,' she said, and without further ado she unzipped the cocktail dress and let it drift silently to the floor. She wasn't wearing a bra, and her breasts were small. She was on the thin side of slender, with a flat tummy and slim legs. She wore black thong panties, no more than a strip of material clinging tightly to her mons, the waistband as thin as string.

'So, you're a real live slave,' she said, coming right up to Andrea and carefully examining her body. She was, Andrea thought, ever so slightly drunk, her speech a little slurred, her co-ordination not quite perfect.

'Yes, mistress,' Andrea intoned.

'Oh don't start all that mistress stuff, please. I'm not sure I'm into any of this.' She sat on the edge of the bed and stared up at Andrea. 'This really turns you on, doesn't it?'

Andrea nodded.

'Incredible. And I can ask you to do anything I want?'

'Yes.' Andrea had a great deal of trouble not

adding, 'mistress'.

'Okay,' Trissie said, her eyes twinkling just a little, 'kneel then.'

Andrea immediately got to her knees. With her hands bound to her throat it was not easy, and she thumped down onto the carpet a little heavily.

'Kiss my feet.' Trissie giggled and pushed a foot up to Andrea's lips. Andrea kissed her toes and licked them. 'Mmm... that's quite nice, I must admit, but I'm not at all turned on.' She replaced her left foot with her right, wriggling her toes right into Andrea's mouth. 'Try sucking them,' she said.

Andrea sucked harder, drawing as much of the foot into her mouth as she could.

'Hey, now that's nice,' Trissie exclaimed at once.

Andrea sucked again and saw the girl shiver.

'I'm going to tell you a little secret,' Trissie whispered conspiratorially. 'I've never ever done it with a woman before. Apart from in the showers at school, I've never even seen a woman naked - I mean, not up close and personal. It's kind of exciting and scary all at the same time. Are you a dike?'

'No,' Andrea said. 'I like men too. It's just that Isabella...'

'Hates men. I know. She told me. So what am I supposed to do now?'

'You can do whatever you want.'

'Lie on the bed.' Despite her apparent reluctance, this order was issued with the same authority as it might have been by Isabella.

Andrea did as she was told, lying back on the cream-coloured counterpane.

Trissie got to her knees beside her. 'Open your legs,' she said, her voice just a little husky. Inquisitively, she examined Andrea's parted thighs, running a hand up along the stockings to the broad band of naked flesh above the stocking top. 'You've great legs,' she whispered. Her wide eyes were riveted to the gusset of the teddy that covered Andrea's sex. 'Am I really going to do this?' she said, almost to herself.

Apparently, the answer was yes. She leant forward and slowly undid the three poppers, then tentatively, almost as though she wasn't sure what to expect, lifted the flimsy, slightly damp material back onto Andrea's unmoving tummy.

'My *God*...' she breathed, in awe, 'you've been shaved. Did Isabella do that?'

Andrea nodded, unable to say a word; such was her mounting arousal beneath the innocent explorations of the girl.

Trissie stroked higher up Andrea's thighs, and quivered visibly as her fingertips glided over the supple flesh of her labia. 'So hot...' she whispered. Gaining confidence, she used her fingers to spread the wet labia apart. Andrea watched her staring.

'That makes me feel all funny in here,' Trissie said, pressing her free hand down against the front of her black panties. She explored a little further and Andrea felt her clitoris respond. Trissie stared, spellbound, and dreamily squirmed her knees apart and slipped her fingers inside her own panties, moaning softly. 'My clit's all swollen and I'm really wet,' she said quietly.

Then, with graceful ease, she slipped out of her panties, moved up the bed a little and lifted a leg over Andrea's shoulders, so her sex was poised just above Andrea's mouth.

'This is the sort of thing we're supposed to do, isn't it?' she asked, with a naivety that really turned

Andrea on.

'Uh-huh,' was all Andrea could mumble, her mouth suddenly dry, the girl's delicious sex beckoning her lips.

Very slowly Trissie lowered herself. 'I love it when men do this to me,' she said sweetly. 'But I guess it's better with a woman.'

Andrea closed her eyes as the girl's sweet sex settled down on her mouth. Unable to do much else, even if she wanted to, Andrea kissed Trissie's pussy lips, greedily thrusting her tongue between them and working it against her clit.

'Oh yes...' Trissie gasped. Andrea found there was enough play in the metal cuffs for her to manoeuvre her fingers to Trissie's sex. She squirmed one and then two into the mouth of her vagina and immediately felt the girl push back on them, urging them deeper.

'This is really good,' Trissie whispered in a tone of astonishment.

Andrea thrust her fingers. Trissie's vagina was lovely and tight, but she managed to ease them right up to the knuckle. She could feel the satiny wet flesh clenching around them with a definite rhythm. The girl's clitoris was throbbing too, so strongly she could feel it against her tongue.

'Bloody hell...' The girl shuddered. She tossed her head from side to side and spread her knees further apart, grinding across Andrea's mouth and pressing down forcefully. 'Bloody *hell*...'

Andrea could feel the muscles in Trissie's lean thighs tense and grip. Trissie instinctively took both her breasts in her hands, pinching her nipples cruelly, her fingernails cutting deep into the puckered flesh. Then she let out a long wailing sigh, her eyes clamped shut and her head flopping back. Andrea felt a flood of juices coating her lips and chin, and savoured the feel of the girl lost in her orgasm.

It took a long time for Trissie to come down. Her back was arched and she was rigid, and she had a glazed look in her eyes, as though suffering from shock. Eventually she collapsed on the bed at Andrea's side, completely enervated.

'Bloody hell...' she mumbled into the mattress, 'that was *so* good. I had no idea... no idea. I've never come like that before. It must be because it's, like, forbidden... you know, a taboo. It feels like it's really sinful. That makes everything so intense.'

But her lack of energy didn't last long. After a few minutes she rose to her knees with alluring agility, staring down at Andrea's body. She leant lower and sucked on the two fingers of Andrea's hand that had penetrated her sex. 'Mmm... I taste good,' she purred. 'But now it's time I think I had a taste of you. Move your legs apart.' This time all hesitancy had gone. Her voice was stern and commanding. 'I could get used to this,' she said, as she dipped her head between Andrea's thighs.

Chapter 7

'All right, I want you to listen very carefully,' Marchessa Isabella Sanchez announced. 'My nephew, Pedro, is arriving today. He is going to stay with me for a week. It was not my idea, but I have to put up with it.'

The slaves were standing in the corridor of the outbuilding where they were housed. Dallas Fox and

Isabella Sanchez stood in front of them.

'During his stay I have arranged for you all to wear uniforms, and you will behave like servants in his presence. You will not address me as mistress. He must not get any clue about what goes on here. Is that understood?'

The girls nodded.

'Pedro is a precocious young man with too much energy to be good for him, and if he tries to make any advances towards you of any sort you are to reject them and report to Dallas or to me. Is that clear?'

Again, the girls nodded.

'Good.' Isabella's eyes became threatening slits. 'Because if I find any of you disobey me it will not merely be a case of punishment. No, you will be sent away immediately and I will make sure you are thrown out of *The System* for ever. That is how seriously I regard this matter.' Her voice was cold and hard. She looked at each girl in turn, her severe expression emphasising what she had said, then walked away, leaving Dallas to stress the point.

Pedro was an attractive young man. He was nineteen or twenty, Andrea guessed, with long black hair and a craggy face, large dark brown eyes, a straight nose, and a sensuous mouth. He was deeply tanned and his muscular build suggested that he exercised regularly in a gym.

Andrea and Carrie had been summoned an hour before. They had been dressed in black maids' uniforms, with short though not immodest skirts and relatively low-heeled shoes. They had been stationed in the sitting room to serve drinks.

'Another glass of champagne?' Dallas Fox asked the confident young man.

'No thanks, I've had quite enough,' he declined, white teeth flashing. 'If you don't mind, I'd rather like to get to bed. I'm terribly tired.'

'It's a long drive from San Sebastian,' Dallas Fox concurred. She was dressed in a businesslike grey suit. 'And I guess the traffic was heavy.'

'It was. So if you'll excuse me.' He had hardly touched the original glass of champagne Andrea had given him.

'No dinner?' Dallas offered, politely but indifferently.

'Do you think I could have some sandwiches in my room? Something simple, like ham. Perhaps one of these young ladies could bring it up for me.' He smiled blatantly towards Andrea. 'A good night's sleep and I'll feel much better.'

'Of course.' Dallas smiled, though there was no warmth in her eyes. 'That'll be no problem.'

Pedro kissed his aunt goodnight and told Dallas it was nice to meet her. He glanced at the two maids, and Andrea thought she detected a glint of something in his eyes. But it was probably her imagination, she thought.

'Shall I show you the way?' Dallas offered, without enthusiasm.

'No, it's all right, I remember,' he said, his gaze still on Andrea. 'Second door on the left.'

He turned and walked out of the room. His footsteps echoed on the marble staircase.

'He's very polite,' Dallas said.

Isabella nodded pensively. 'I'm surprised,' she said. 'My brother told me he was a bit of a tearaway. Perhaps he's calmed down now. He seems perfectly charming.' She turned to the two girls. 'Go to the kitchen and prepare his sandwiches. Andrea, you can take them up to him.'

Ten minutes later Andrea, carrying a tray with salad, sandwiches, a bottle of wine and a small bowl of fruit, was knocking on Pedro's door.

'Come in,' he called.

She opened the door and walked in. It felt distinctly strange not to be in some form of bondage.

Pedro was standing by the bed. He was wearing a pair of black silk briefs, so minuscule they barely covered his genitals. His body, and particularly his chest and legs, were covered in thick black hair and was just as muscular as Andrea had imagined. He had a broad chest, a flat well-defined abdomen, and his arms and legs were contoured by hard muscle.

'Put it down over there,' he said, indicating a chest of drawers by one wall. Andrea did as she was told. 'What's your name?'

She told him politely.

'Nice. Where are you from?' He sat on the edge of the bed. His expensive gold watch caught the light from the bedside lamp.

'England, sir.'

'That's where I went to school. All members of the Sanchez family are sent to school in England.' It explained his faultless English. 'You're a very beautiful woman, Andrea,' he added.

'Thank you, sir,' she said with a little blush. 'Now, I think I'd better be going.'

'Oh, come on now. Don't be difficult. I only agreed to come here so I could play with the slaves.'

Andrea's mouth fell open in surprise. 'I don't know what you mean,' she said. Isabella's words of warning were ringing in her ears.

'I know my aunt likes to pretend, but I know what goes on here. I know all about it. You are a slave, aren't you?' Andrea lowered her eyes and nodded. Pedro grinned. 'Then you must obey me,' he said confidently. 'Come here. Let's find out what you've got on under that dress.'

'No,' Andrea objected. 'I mustn't. We're all forbidden to...'

'All? How many are there?'

'Six.'

'And you've all been warned not to talk to me and tell me about Aunt Isabella's wonderful secrets?'

Andrea nodded again. 'And we're not allowed to... to...'

'Play with me?' Pedro laughed. With amazing speed he lunged off the bed, caught Andrea by the hand and pulled her into his arms, kissing her full on the mouth. After so much female flesh, after weeks of being embraced by the supple body of a woman, Pedro's muscular torso crushing against her felt wonderful, his arms holding her like steel bands. As his tongue explored her mouth Andrea felt herself swooning with pleasure.

'N-no,' she managed, pulling away. After all her conditioning with Charles Hawksworth and her training with Marie-Claire it went against her instincts to disobey, but she knew she had to.

'Come back here, you little bitch! I haven't finished with you.' Pedro caught her by the hand again but she managed to twist her wrist free and scamper to the door. She ran along the corridor and down the stairs. Pedro did not pursue her, no doubt worried in case his aunt might see.

She should have gone straight to Isabella, of course. That was what she had been instructed to do if Pedro behaved in the way he had. But she was frightened. Though she had no idea where he'd got his information, Pedro appeared to know all his aunt's proclivities. If she told Isabella what had happened she might not believe that he knew all about the slaves already, and blame her for somehow blurting it out. And that was not a risk she was prepared to take. Not with the ultimate punishment hanging over her head like a sword of Damocles.

Instead, she said nothing. And that was her real mistake.

Andrea was startled awake. She listened carefully and tried to hear what had woken her, then realised it was the key turning in the lock. As no light spilt into the room as the door was opened she guessed it was still the middle of the night.

'Shh...' a voice said in a whisper. It was Pedro.

'W-what are you doing here?' Andrea stammered.

'Isn't that obvious?'

'How did you find me?'

'I asked for more wine. The other girl brought it up to me. She was much more co-operative, but less pretty. I wanted you. She told me where to find you.'

He sat on the edge of the bed.

'You've got to leave,' Andrea insisted fearfully.

'Why?' he taunted. 'Are you going to raise the alarm? I don't think so. If you were going to do that you'd have told Isabella what I did when you brought the sandwiches and I'd probably already be on my way out. But you didn't, did you?'

Andrea didn't respond, her heart thumping in her chest.

'And why not?' he proceeded anyway.

'You - you're not supposed to know anything about all this. I was scared she'd blame me for telling you.'

He chuckled. 'I'm sure she would.'

'How did you find out?'

'I happened to be going out with this girl who mentioned that she'd met the Marchessa. She didn't know she was my aunt. Apparently Isabella propositioned her, asked her if she'd be interested in becoming a slave. She showed her around the castle. The girl was really into women and she was happy to go to bed with Isabella, but she wasn't sure if she was into submission.'

He stood up. He was wearing slacks and a shirt. He began unbuttoning his shirt.

Andrea shook her head, her eyes fixed on his moving fingers. 'Please, if she finds me with you...'

'You haven't a choice,' he silenced her. 'If you refuse I'll go to my aunt and tell her you told me all about the slaves and how terribly upset and shocked I am. Do you want me to do that?'

It was the second time she had been blackmailed at the castle, and once again she knew she had no choice but to comply.

'All right, I'll do whatever you want,' she whispered. 'But not here.'

'Why not?'

'The walls are thin. We're bound to wake the other girls. It only takes one of them to report us...'

'All right,' he said suspiciously, 'where?'

'There's a soundproofed room at the end of the corridor.'

He gazed towards the door, for the first time looking a little indecisive. 'Okay...' he eventually said, 'show me.'

Andrea had mixed feelings as she got to her feet. She was very scared. If Isabella discovered what she was doing after giving a specific warning against it, she would have no defence. Pedro was family and she was unlikely to believe her instead of him. But the fact that her pulse was racing and her heart pounding was not entirely due to fear. The brief physical encounter with Pedro earlier had left her flustered with desire. She had been unable to forget the way his virile body had crushed against hers and had spent most of the evening thinking about him.

'This way,' she whispered. She carefully closed and locked the door of her room, then led him down to the far end of the corridor. 'In here,' she said, unlocking the last door.

She relaxed slightly once they were inside and she had bolted the heavily padded door behind them. Unless someone discovered she was not in her room they would be safe.

'Well, look at this.' Pedro was staring at the chains and ropes. He went to the chest of drawers and opened each drawer, examining the contents carefully. 'So this is where all the kinky stuff goes on, is that right?'

Andrea nodded.

He unbuttoned his shirt and kicked off his loafers. He wasn't wearing socks. He pulled down his trousers and briefs, and stepped out of them. He had tight buttocks and a circumcised cock that was already beginning to engorge. The pubic hair that surrounded it was thick, curly and black.

'Come over here,' he said. He caught her by the wrist and pulled her into his arms, very much as he had done earlier. But the impact was much greater. As their naked bodies crushed together and he kissed her Andrea felt a huge jolt of desire. She could feel his cock swelling rapidly against her belly.

'Please,' she panted, despite herself. She could kid herself that what she'd done with Dallas was not actually disobedience, since Isabella had never expressly told her it was forbidden. But this was entirely different. This was direct disobedience.

'Please, what?' he goaded.

'Please...' she said again, 'let me go.'

He laughed. 'You don't really want that. I can feel it. I know what you want.'

The trouble was, he was right. His now fully erect cock was pressing into her belly and she wanted desperately to feel it up inside her. It had been so long since she'd had a man, even to touch and hold, that her juices were already lubricating her. Her nipples, too, had knotted into hard pebbles and her clit was pulsing hungrily.

'Tie me up, then,' she begged. 'Tie me to the bed - anything.' If she were bound, if she were unable to stop him taking advantage of her, that would make her feel better and absolve her of guilt. And it was, after all, a reflection of the truth. However much she desired him she told herself she would not be in the room with him if he hadn't threatened to tell Isabella a downright lie.

'I think I'd like that,' he leered appreciatively, looking around the room. The plain wooden double bed had leather cuffs attached to each corner. 'Go and lie on that,' he ordered, his voice thickening with excitement.

Andrea did as she was told. She lay in the middle of the white sheet and stretched her arms and legs across it towards the cuffs.

Pedro stood looking down on her, his threatening erection spearing from his belly. After a few tense minutes he knelt on the edge of the mattress and buckled her left wrist into a padded cuff, then moved around the bed and secured all her limbs one by one. The chains that fastened the cuffs to the frame were short, and by the time he'd finished Andrea was stretched taut.

'Completely helpless,' Pedro mused, looking down at her again. He knelt at her side. Cool fingertips stroked her nearest cheek. 'Now you can pretend I force you, is that it?' he said thickly.

'You are forcing me,' she countered.

He laughed. 'You are the slave and I am your master. Is that the game you play?'

Andrea closed her eyes against his taunting and said nothing. She ached with desire. The tight bondage had only added to the arousal she felt.

'Then call me master,' he demanded.

He was not her master in the true sense, but the merest thought of the word produced a thrilling surge of excitement in the pit of her tummy. 'Yes... master...' she sighed.

He stroked her cheek then ran his fingertips down her throat to her breasts, squeezing the vulnerable flesh then pinching her nipples. She moaned and rolled her head to one side.

'This is very exciting,' he said. His hand ran down over her trembling belly. 'How often are you shaved?' he asked as he caressed between her thighs.

'Every... every day, master.' That word again. She relished it. However much pleasure she'd had with Isabella she would never be able to feel the same about a woman as she felt about a man. She arched her buttocks off the bed and angled her sex up towards Pedro, hoping he would take the hint. The desire she felt was so extreme it was painful. Why didn't he just throw himself on top of her and fuck her? How could he resist?

A finger slid between her labia, nudging against her pulsing clit.

'You're very wet,' he said hoarsely. 'Why is that?' He was playing with her.

'Because... because I want you, master.' He tapped his finger against the little bud and Andrea cried out. Every nerve in her body was wired and this tiny movement produced a huge wave of desire. 'Please... don't torture me,' she begged, her head rolling slowly from side to side between her tensed shoulders.

'I thought torture is what slaves enjoy.' Pedro moved his finger over her clit, caressing it delicately. He moved so he was kneeling near Andrea's head, then leant forward, his cock pulsing over her flushed face. She could see a tear of clear fluid oozing from the tip. 'If you want it so much, suck it for me,' he encouraged huskily.

As though in a dream, Andrea raised her head and pressed her lips around the smooth helmet. She sucked hard, her cheeks hollowing. His cock throbbed in response, jerking up against the roof of her mouth.

'You're very good at that,' he croaked, pulling away.

He pushed his fingers lower and they sunk into Andrea's vagina. She gasped, her labia closing around it.

'Please...' she begged him. She could imagine exactly how it would feel to have that circumcised penis plunging into the depths of her cunt. She didn't think she had ever wanted anything more in her life.

Suddenly Pedro rolled on top of her. In one fluid movement he bucked his hips and drove his cock straight up into her vagina, filling her completely, his glans buried in the neck of her womb. Andrea cried out, every sense concentrated on his bludgeoning cock. But as the tight tube of her sex clenched around it she felt it already beginning to jerk convulsively.

Pedro pulled back, thrust his cock up into her one more time, and came, jets of boiling spunk spattering out of his spasming cock. His whole body shook violently on top of her, his mouth pressed to her throat, his chest pressing down against her breasts. Andrea's excitement died. She felt his cock soften and the sticky sap of his ejaculation already beginning to seep out from her vagina.

'That was really something,' he eventually grunted.

She felt him nibble wearily at the flesh of her neck. He worked up to her ear, then he raised his head and kissed her on the mouth. At the same time he worked a hand between their bodies and took hold of her right breast, lifting himself slightly so he could knead the flesh. He rolled her nipple between his fingers.

'Lovely,' he sighed. She saw his eyes looking at her arms, their sinews stretched taut by the tight bondage. He began moving his hips, almost imperceptibly at first, and in a matter of seconds she was amazed to feel him beginning to stiffen again. As he thrust his hips more forcibly his cock grew harder and harder.

The feel of him swelling inside her instantly renewed her desire. The rhythm of his hips increased. He let go of her breast and slid his hands to her sides, supporting himself as he drove into her, pounding her with his considerable strength. She could feel the hard muscles of his belly pushing down on her own and the muscles of his thighs driving him forward.

Her own body was not slow to respond. All the desire she had felt before returned with renewed vigour. As he thrust himself up into her he ground the base of his phallus against her clit, making it leap with sensation.

She was coming. After weeks of not having a man, of being penetrated only by plastic or rubber phalluses, the feeling of a voracious and animate length of cock was simply overwhelming.

'Ohhh...' she cried, wrenching her limbs against the bonds that held them so tightly, wanting to feel that constriction too, everything adding to her arousal. Despite his weight she managed to thrust herself up off the bed towards him, driving him deeper and deeper. And that was enough. Her orgasm broke over the smooth, silky skin of his glans, a wave of the most intense sensations coursing through every nerve in her body. But he did not stop. Though she was sure he must have felt her contracting around him, gripping him as tightly as any fist, he continued to plough into her. As soon as her first orgasm had ebbed the relentless pounding she was taking produced another, an orgasm that blossomed as quickly as any she'd ever had. And still he drove on. She thought she could feel every vein and ridge on his cock and she was sure it was still swelling, its size increasing with every thrust. It made noisy squelchings as it plunged into her.

Then he stopped. He thrust up into her but instead of pulling back used every muscle to try and push deeper, his buttocks as hard as steel, his whole body locked. As Andrea felt her sex close around him tightly in a reflexive movement he was suddenly completely still - so still she thought she could hear his heartbeat. That moment seemed to go on forever. Then he made an odd choking sound. At that moment she felt his cock jerk. Immediately a jet of spunk lashed into her body, as hot and as copious as his first spending had been.

Eventually it was over and he raised his head from her shoulder. 'What do you say?' he drawled, grinning lethargically.

'Thank you, master.' Andrea didn't think she had ever meant anything so sincerely in her whole life.

'We've got to be quiet,' Andrea insisted anxiously.
'Everyone's in bed,' Pedro reassured.
'We mustn't get caught.'
'We won't.'
The two moved stealthily along the corridor to the small dark blue room and bolted its thickly padded door behind them.

Pedro had visited her every night for the last four nights, his infatuation with her growing ever greater. He had rifled through the castle surreptitiously and found a wardrobe where Isabella stored many of the outrageous outfits the slaves would be made to wear, and had brought one of them with him every night. His taste was for extremely tight garments, in leather or rubber. He had found the ultra high heels they were made to wear too.

'Here,' he said, handing her the bundle he was carrying. 'Put this on.'
'Yes, master,' she said obediently.
He had brought a shiny black rubber corset, stockings in the same material, and ankle boots in black patent leather.

As Andrea began to wrestle the tight rubber up over her body, Pedro pulled off the black silk robe he was wearing. He was naked underneath, his cock already slightly engorged. He went to the chest of drawers. He had investigated its contents on their first visit and by now knew everything it contained. Over the last four nights it was not only his desire to have her dressed in outre outfits that had evolved rapidly, but his taste for bondage and domination. After their first encounter he seemed to have become increasingly fascinated with playing the role of her master, and had insisted each night that she was bound and constricted more and more severely.

He took two thin straps and two leather cuffs from the top drawer, then sat on the edge of the bed and watched Andrea struggling into the rubber. The corset reached down over her buttocks. It had wide shoulder straps and short stubby suspenders, and there were small holes in the bra that allowed her nipples to poke through.

The rubber stockings were even more difficult to get on. Andrea sat on the bed and pulled and tugged them up her long legs while Pedro watched, his eyes glinting with excitement. Finally, with both stockings clinging tightly, she stood up and smoothed out the last of the creases, before clipping them into the suspenders.

'Very good,' Pedro said. 'Now put your hands out in front of you. I have to strap them together.'

Andrea obeyed. One of the leather straps was wrapped around her crossed wrists. He buckled it tight, making the leather bite into her flesh.

'I like to see this,' he said. 'Now put your feet up on the edge of the bed.'

As Andrea obeyed again, Pedro strapped the leather cuffs around her ankles.

'Over here now,' he continued. He led her to the centre of the room, where the two thick leather straps hung down from the metal bar. He adjusted the loops so they were low enough for Andrea to put her legs through. 'Come on then,' he said impatiently, 'what are you waiting for?'

Andrea raised her legs and slid them into the leather loops, sitting in them as though they were a swing. Pedro pulled her arms up to the metal bar and bound her wrists to it with the second strap. Then he pulled her ankles up behind her and clipped a double-ended snaphook already attached to a D-ring in the leather cuff to a similar fitting on the loop of leather underneath her thigh. With her feet pulled off the floor Andrea began to swing slightly back and forth.

He stood back to admire his work. His cock had grown during the process and was now jutting aggressively from his groin. He went back to the chest of drawers and took out a short whip. It was identical to the one Dallas had used on her breasts; countless thin lashes bound into a braided handle.

'Open your legs,' Pedro said, with a cruel smile. His enjoyment of sadism was obvious. Perhaps it was a family trait.

Andrea pulled her knees apart, knowing perfectly well what he was going to do. She had no choice but to obey. Had she gone to Isabella and told her the truth she was quite sure that Pedro would be able to twist whatever she said and it would all end up being her fault. He would tell his aunt that not only had she given him all the details of what went on at the castle, but had seduced him and encouraged him into being her master. It was perfectly plausible, after all. Isabella knew most of her slaves were not lesbians and found it hard to be constantly reminded of sex and all things sexual without being able to enjoy the services of a man. She would put it down to Andrea's frustration.

But despite her anxiety and the fear of discovery, the last four days had also been incredibly exciting. Pedro's remarkable libido had been demonstrated over and over again. He seemed indefatigable, and the way he treated her was wonderful too. The more he assumed the role of the master, the more she responded. Though she knew everything they did together was wrong, that she was disobeying her real master, she could not deny the excitement she felt. Bound once again and completely helpless, she could already feel the familiar thrill deep in her sex.

Pedro raised his arm, aiming the whip between her legs. It made a whistling noise as it sliced through the air, the thin lashes flicking against her sex, like a thousand cuts. She cried out, her face contorted.

This only encouraged Pedro. 'Yes, I like this. Let's hear you again.'

The whip cut down, harder this time. The lashes swiped against her labia, curling around the tender flesh. She winced.

'Good, more, more.' He gave her three more strokes in quick succession, her body swaying in the creaking leather harness. Her sex was stinging. The lashes seemed to invade every part of it, cutting up between her labia. But she was not wincing with pain any more, but panting for breath. She would never understand the mechanism that turned pain into the extraordinary pleasure she was feeling now, a pleasure so intense it literally took her breath away. She knew she was going to come. Somehow the tightness of the rubber corset wrapped around her body increased everything she felt, as though her feelings were trapped and could not leech away.

Pedro turned his attention to her breasts. He sliced the whip down on them, the tiny lashes catching her exposed nipples and turning to fire. But again the pain rapidly turned to pleasure and her breasts began to throb with the tempo that was affecting the rest of her body.

After six or seven strokes on each breast Pedro threw the whip aside. He came up behind her and wrapped his arms around her body, his erect cock sliding between her buttocks. 'This is what you love, isn't it slave?' he panted.

'Yes, master.' It was. She had loved it from the moment Charles Hawksworth had first put her into bondage and whipped her. It had given her life a new dimension. 'Yes, master, it is.'

His hands moved to her breasts, squeezing the rubber covered flesh and pinching her nipples. 'Tell me,' he demanded. For the last four nights he had insisted she tell him as she orgasmed.

'I - I'm coming, master...'

'Yes, you are,' he said smugly. 'Let me feel it.'

Her body shuddered. Her labia clenched around the upper surface of his cock, her clit spasmed and her orgasm burst. She cried, throwing her head back against his shoulder. In the suspension of the leather harness she felt as if she was floating, giving her climax an almost unreal sensation.

If he were her real master he would have warned her that she must not come without permission. But he was not. He did not know about that particular torment yet. But that did not mean she felt guiltless. She knew perfectly well that everything she had done with Pedro was the worst sort of disobedience. But though she was sure Isabella would not believe her if she told her how it had all happened, her own guilt was assuaged by the knowledge that none of this was really of her making. Whatever Isabella would think, it was not her fault that she was in this situation.

As her orgasm ebbed away she felt Pedro angling his cock up between her sex lips. He paused briefly as his glans nosed into the mouth of her vagina, greeted by a spasm of the soft wet flesh, then used his strength to power up into her with such force he lifted her out of the leather loops.

Reflexively her vagina clenched around him. He began to move, pumping in and out of her, holding her by the hips, pulling her back onto him as he pushed forward. His cock was as hard as a rod of steel. But it was hot too, and bathed in her juices.

Andrea wrestled to control her emotions as his pounding thrusts created wave after wave of intense pleasure. But then she felt him pull right out of her. His hands held her steady and his cock nosed up into the cleft of her buttocks, his glans pressing against her sphincter.

'I haven't fucked you here yet,' he grunted, pressing forward. There was only momentary resistance from the little ring of muscles, then his glans forged into her tight rear passage. The pulsing sensation in the depths of her cunt, that was the precursor of orgasm, stirred yet again. It melded with a similar sensation in her bottom, and with the throbbing spasms of her clit. In seconds, in less than seconds, she was on the very brink of an orgasm again.

But so was Pedro. She felt his cock flex and swell. The extra girth as his spunk pumped up from his balls temporarily revived the discomfort she'd felt as he'd invaded her, stretching her anus around him still tighter. And he thrust forward more forcefully too, penetrating her until she could feel his pubic hair grinding against her buttocks. But the pain only intensified her pleasure and as she felt him spasming and the first gobs of spunk spattered into her, she came too, her body closing around him, sealing him into her.

For long minutes they remained locked together, the only sounds in the room their slowing breathing and the rhythmic creak of the leather harness. At last he pulled away, his limp cock glistening in the half-light.

Andrea swung gently in the leather straps. She shuddered, still feeling the aftermath of her orgasm.

Pedro went to the wall and operated the switch that lowered the metal bar. There was a whine of electric motors and Andrea descended until she was kneeling on the floor. But he made no attempt to untie her. Instead, he sat on the edge of the bed.

'I have decided,' he said. 'I have only two more days here, and then I must leave. I want you to come with me.'

'Come with you?' So replete was Andrea, she wasn't really taking in his words.

'Yes, come with me,' he confirmed. 'My family is very wealthy. They have bought me a house in Madrid. I've stayed here awaiting the finishing touches. Now it is ready. It will be ideal. Private. Good security. I want you to come with me. I will be your master.'

Andrea shook her head wearily. 'No,' she said, her awareness slowly returning.

'No?' he scoffed. 'What do you mean, no? You are a slave. You need a master. I will be your master. You cannot refuse.'

'Pedro, you don't understand...'

'If you do not address me as master I will understand that I have to whip you again!' he threatened.

'But I can't leave here, master,' she pleaded, realising the seriousness of his intentions.

'Oh, don't worry about my aunt,' he snorted dismissively. 'I'll smuggle you out in the boot of my car. She'll never know it was me. She'll think you decided to escape.'

'Exactly - and I can't do that. They'll throw me out

of *The System*.'

'System? What system?'

'I'm a slave. My master - my first master - is in England. He had me trained. I had to agree to be sent to a new master for six months. Your aunt chose me, and for the moment she is my mistress. I think she had to pay for me - probably quite a lot of money. If I do not obey, if I tried to escape, I would be punished by being sent back home and being thrown out of *The System*. My master is responsible for me. He would never forgive me.'

'But none of that matters,' Pedro said, ignoring her reasoning. 'I will be your master. Just like I have been these last four nights. I will treat you as a slave. I will learn how to be a real master.' He smiled. 'I might even find other girls for you to play with. I would like that, watching you with another girl.'

'No, please master. It's impossible.'

'Andrea, it is my understanding that slaves do not contradict their masters.'

'But you are not my master!' she argued desperately.

Pedro's eyes narrowed as he stared at her. 'I think that outburst deserves a punishment, don't you?' he said quietly.

'Please, Pedro.' It was the first time she'd used his name. 'Please, this is not a game for me. I am committed to *The System*. I don't want to be expelled from it. I promised my master - my real master - that I would be obedient. You forced me to do all this.'

'You will be *my* slave.'

'No!'

'Perhaps I should leave you here and let Isabella find you,' Pedro threatened. 'Perhaps I should tell her what we have done.'

'No, please.' His obsession was alarming Andrea. 'You don't understand. I'm not a free agent. I can't just do what I want.' The four nights she had spent with Pedro had been incredibly exciting; he was an attractive man and an amazing lover. But it did not occur to her for one moment to accept his offer. She belonged to Charles Hawksworth. Everything she did, she did for him.

Pedro got to his feet. He moved around in front of her and wrapped a hand around her neck. 'I should punish you,' he warned. 'I should string you up again and whip you until you beg me to stop.'

'Yes, master,' she said, trying to appease him. 'Whatever you want.'

'Open your mouth,' he snapped sternly, 'your master commands it.'

Andrea knew there was nothing else she could do. Her moist lips peeled obediently apart and he fed his flaccid cock between them. She sucked him, hoping to make him forget his devious schemes. She knew he would be able to ejaculate again. His cock began to grow almost immediately. She ran her tongue around his glans and felt it swell. In seconds he was erect again and stretching her lips wide apart, and she could feel the prominent veins of the gnarled length beginning to throb.

Andrea bobbed her head back and forth, sinking upon him until his glans was buried in the back of her throat, then pulling right back until her lips were pursed around his glans. As he slid back inside she used her tongue to massage the whole length of him. She felt a secret triumphant rush; she knew there was nothing he could do to expedite his plan. There was no hope of him being able to get her out of the castle undetected. If he tried she could scream and fight and raise the alarm. There was little doubt that Isabella would take an entirely different view of his conduct if she saw for herself that he was trying to smuggle one of the slaves away.

'I'm going to come deep in your throat now,' he hissed above her, his tone angry and cold. His fingers clamped onto her head and he thrust his groin aggressively against her beleaguered face. Andrea closed her eyes, Pedro stiffened and grunted like a dying animal, and her mouth filled with his salty ejaculation.

Chapter 8

In order not to compromise the secrets of the castle during her nephew's visit, Isabella had made sure there were no guests to call on the services of the slaves, so Andrea had no night-time activities to break up the monotony of her domestic chores. And, since she had turned down his offer, she had not seen Pedro either. For the last two nights the door to her room had remained firmly closed and locked.

It was a relief. She had sworn to Charles Hawksworth that she would obey her new master and her repeated disobedience had caused her great anxiety, despite the intense pleasure Pedro's nocturnal visits had given her. She was glad it was over. Pedro had either decided to try and inveigle one of the other girls into becoming his house slave, or had gone into Madrid for his nightly entertainment. Either way, it appeared he had accepted her rejection, though probably, knowing him, not with good grace.

On the final day of his visit Andrea had been

assigned the duty of serving breakfast, the modest black dress and low-heeled shoes maintaining the fiction of her status as a servant.

She had wondered how Pedro would react to her presence, but she need not have worried. He totally ignored her.

'Have some more coffee,' Isabella said to him. Breakfast had been served on a small terrace that faced south, a canopy of bougainvillaea dripping from overhead trellising.

'No, I must get into the city by eleven,' he declined politely. 'I'm meeting an old school friend for lunch. My cases are in the hall, so I'm all ready to go.'

'I'll get Dallas to bring your car around to the front.'

Pedro dabbed his lips with a crisp napkin and rose smoothly. 'It's been a very enjoyable visit,' he said.

'I look forward to seeing your new home.'

'You will be my first guest, I promise.'

Isabella stood up too. He took her hand and kissed her on both cheeks. 'And you must not be a stranger now you're living so close,' she said. 'I hope you'll come and see me often.'

'I will, don't worry.'

They walked back into the house. Almost immediately Andrea heard the throaty sound of a sports car being driven up to the front door. A few minutes later it accelerated off, growling noisily.

'Clear up here.' Dallas Fox had appeared on the terrace. She was wearing a white silk slip dress, with narrow straps. It floated over her voluptuous body, emphasising her flawless tan.

Andrea began to load the dirty dishes onto a tray. Dallas came up behind, deliberately pushing against her.

'Now Pedro's gone normal service can be resumed,' she said conspiratorially. She slipped a hand around Andrea and squeezed her breasts. 'I've missed you. You're special. You know that, don't you?'

Andrea remained still, holding her breath.

'Well you are,' Dallas answered her own question, her fresh breath making the soft hair over Andrea's ear dance lightly in the crisp morning light. 'Isabella knows it too. She wants to keep you all to herself. I'm on strict instructions not to go near you.' Dallas smiled to herself - a smile of cunning. 'But Isabella is going away for a few days and nights, so what the eye doesn't see...' She laughed suggestively. 'I'm feeling very dominant at the moment. I've been imagining what I'll do to you. You haven't been whipped for days. Have you missed it?'

Andrea remained silent. Fortunately the marks from the whipping by Pedro had faded away.

'Have you?' Dallas insisted, pinching her nipple to emphasise the need for a reply.

'Yes, Ms Fox,' Andrea whispered, 'I have missed it.'

'Good, because tonight I'm going to string you up and give you a good hiding. And there's lots of time for the marks to heal before Isabella gets back.' Her hand dropped to Andrea's buttocks. It forced its way down between her legs, dragging the material of the dress with it and making Andrea adjust her stance a little, until it was rubbing against her sex. Isabella's efforts to give the appearance of respectability to her slaves did not include panties. For a moment Andrea felt persistent fingers, cocooned in the material of her short dress, pushing up into her. 'Perhaps I'll bring one of the other girls with me to help. I might even borrow one of Isabella's strap-on dildos.' The fingers withdrew and Dallas moved away. 'See you later,' she said.

The rest of the day passed slowly. Perhaps because she wanted to rest Andrea for the evening's activities she had in mind, Dallas returned her to her room after lunch rather than working her through the day. Andrea lay on her bed, and before she realised what had happened, fell asleep.

She woke placidly, drifting in an out of sleep. She thought she heard a car pulling out of the courtyard and imagined it was Isabella departing. She didn't think it would be long before Dallas arrived.

She had slept soundly and had no idea what time it was. The outbuildings were quiet. None of the other girls made a sound and there were no comings or goings, so it might have been later than she thought.

Then the oddest thing happened. She heard a faint knocking sound. It was so faint it could have been coming from any of the doors in the corridor, but Andrea was sure it was coming from hers. She got up off the bed and moved stealthily over to the door, and listened intently.

'Who is it?' she whispered, completely puzzled. The key was kept in the lock on the outside. If someone wanted to come in they only had to unlock the door.

Three taps this time, light and almost inaudible.

'Please - who is it?' Andrea repeated hesitantly.

Suddenly she heard the key turn and the door burst open. She jumped back in surprise but an arm caught her waist while a hand clamped firmly over her mouth, stifling a scream. Two strong arms swung her around and a black velvet bag was pulled down over her head, cutting out all light. She'd barely glimpsed the two figures that had burst into her room. There was a drawstring on the bag and she felt it being tightened around her throat.

Then she heard the door being shut.

'Hey, she's really something. Look at that body.' It was a man's voice. He spoke English with only the slightest of Spanish accents.

'All right, get the gag ready.' This voice she recognised. It was Pedro!

She struggled, trying to pull the arm from around her waist, but could make no impression on the steel hard muscles. She felt the hand over her mouth being withdraw, but just as she was about to scream, a solid ball was pushed against her lips, forcing it and the velvet into her mouth.

'Tie it tight,' Pedro hissed.

Andrea felt a strap being fastened around the back of her head.

'Now get her on the floor.'

Hands grasped her ankles. She tried to kick out, but they were much too strong. She was lifted off her feet and laid flat on the floor, her naked body rolled over onto her stomach. A heavy weight descended on her buttocks, holding her down as her arms were yanked behind her back and she felt cold metal handcuffs being clipped tightly around her wrists. Then a strap was wound around her elbows, forcing her shoulders back.

'That's it. Now her legs.'

The weight on her buttocks did not move. She felt a rope being wound around her legs just above her knees. It was jerked tight as it was knotted. More rope was wound around her ankles.

'*Voila*!' Pedro exclaimed triumphantly. The weight lifted. He had been sitting on her.

Andrea tried to struggle free but the bondage was

simple and effective. A foot hooked under her hip and rolled her over onto her back.

'She's great!' the unknown voice enthused, panting heavily from the exertion.

'Didn't I tell you?' Pedro gloated.

'I'm getting a piece of her,' the unknown said. Was he the school friend Pedro had referred to? His English was so good he had definitely been educated in England.

'Of course you will; once she realises who her master is she'll behave like a perfect little slave. Won't you Andrea?' He rubbed the toe of a shoe against Andrea's hip. She cursed hopelessly into the gag and shook her head defiantly. Pedro was not her master - and never would be.

'She doesn't seem too convinced.'

'Don't worry,' Pedro said, his heavy breathing calming, 'she'll be as good as gold - trust me. Now come on, we can't hang around here.'

'How did you get the keys?' the unknown asked.

'That's the funny part.' Pedro chuckled. 'The castle is locked and alarmed but this annex doesn't have any security. It's designed to keep the girls in, not keep anyone out.'

'Come on then, I can't wait to get her back to your place.'

Andrea felt hands lifting her off the floor. Then she was tilted back over a broad shoulder, her head hanging down the man's back. She didn't think it was Pedro; the man felt much bigger and bulkier. He appeared not to find her weight any encumbrance and walked out of the room as if he were carrying a feather pillow.

'This way,' Pedro whispered.

Instead of turning down the walkway to the

courtyard they crept in the other direction. The flagstones gave way to grass and Andrea felt that they were descending a steep incline.

'There it is,' Pedro said.

After no more than three or four minutes, the incline straightened up and Andrea heard something solid underfoot. Almost immediately a car door was being opened. She was dropped on her back on the rear seat, then gently lowered to the floor. The car had a thick carpet and a luxurious smell.

Other doors opened and were closed quietly. The engine started up. It was not the roar of Pedro's car, but a much quieter purr.

'I found that door when I was staying there,' Pedro informed his colleague, and then roared with laughter. 'I'd better tell my aunt to fit it with a lock!'

'Don't do that,' the unknown urged. 'I might want to sneak back and get a girl for myself.'

They laughed together. As they drove down the mountain they began to sing in Spanish, but neither of them had noticed a shadowy figure that had followed them down from the outbuildings and watched from the gate in the castle wall as they drove away.

Andrea had no idea what she was going to do. She was terribly uncomfortable on the floor of the car. The metal cuffs had been snapped too tightly around her wrists and the weave of the rope was cutting into her legs. Her arms, held so tautly behind her back, had already numbed and the fact that the gag had been pushed into her mouth on top of the velvet meant her saliva had soaked much of the material, making it clammy against her face. But it was not the pain that bothered her most. She had been in worse bondage than this in the last few months, and found it exciting.

What worried her was her future.

Instead of turning his attention elsewhere, as she thought he had been doing for the last two days, Pedro had obviously been planning to abduct her and had coerced his friend to help. But he must have thought beyond that too, and prepared quarters for her which, as he must know she would not agree to stay with him of her own free will after her flat rejection of his offer at the castle, needed to be escape proof.

But even supposing his preparations had not been that meticulous, not thinking beyond the initial kidnapping, and Andrea managed to free herself, getting back to the castle was another matter. Pedro would only have to call Isabella and tell her that Andrea had seduced him, begging him to take her away, and there was little doubt that his doting aunt would believe him. Had they caught him in the act as they carried Andrea out of the grounds, bound and struggling, it would be different. But they hadn't. The future looked bleak.

The car must have entered the suburbs of Madrid. It had slowed and occasionally came to a halt altogether, at what Andrea imagined were traffic lights. Eventually she felt it turn left, mount a steep incline and stop. The car doors opened and fresh, rather chilled air wafted in. Andrea was pulled by her feet out of the car, then hoisted up on the man's shoulder again. He gripped her tightly and began walking down a short flight of steps. A door opened with a rattle of keys and Andrea felt warmer air enveloping her. Another door opened and she was lowered onto what felt like a narrow bed.

'Good,' Pedro said. 'Help me untie her.

Fingers unknotted the ropes on her ankles. But before they moved up to the rope around her knees, she felt a metal cuff being clipped around her left ankle. Only when this was secure did they move to untie the second rope. They were obviously being careful to make sure she had not the slightest chance of escape.

With her left leg secured to the bed by the cuff they rolled her onto her stomach and released the leather strap around her elbows. She heard the handcuffs being snapped open, but her arms were much too weak and numb to mount any resistance as they moved her onto her back and pulled them above her head, clipping metal cuffs around her wrists so they were secured to the top corners of the narrow bed. Finally her right ankle was cuffed too. An unforgiving hand rolled her head to one side and undid the strap of the gag. She forced the ball out and tried to ease the ache in her jaw. Though there was some light leaking in through the bottom of the black bag, she could still see nothing.

'We'll let her rest now.'

'I'll come back tomorrow,' the other man said.

'You do that - then we can have some *real* fun and games.'

Andrea heard a noise that sounded as if they were embracing, slapping each other on the back. Then a door creaked and closed.

Pedro leant forward, loosened the drawstring and pulled the bag from her head. She was sweaty, and her long blonde hair was plastered to her rosy forehead and cheeks. She flinched and screwed her eyes shut against the harsh glare of a single light bulb. After a few seconds she gingerly opened her eyes again, and found she was lying on a wooden single bed in a tiny room with white walls. One wall was lined with horizontal bars, rather like those found in a gymnasium. There was a single archway, and beyond she could see a shower cubicle. There were two long narrow windows right at the top of the walls, both made from thick and frosted glass blocks.

'This was going to be my personal gym and shower room,' Pedro announced proudly. 'Convenient isn't it? I'm sure you'll be very happy here.'

'Let me go, Pedro, please,' she said feebly.

'But my dear girl, I've only just got you here,' he mocked.

He sat on the edge of the bed and pulled strains of her hair away from her face with almost tender care.

'Please, Pedro, this is not what I want,' she persisted.

'But I know that it is. You need a man, Andrea. I know that. You need a real man to be your master. I know you very well, I know what you need.' He laughed. 'And here I am to give it to you.' His hand moved down her body and caressed her breasts. 'I have been busy these last two days. I have bought equipment and clothes, just like at the castle. You will see. You will soon learn that to be my slave is the best thing for you.'

'No...' Andrea protested hopelessly.

Pedro stood again. 'You are *my* slave now, and you will obey me,' he said, with studied sternness. He turned and walked out of the room without giving her a second look. She heard a key being turned in the lock.

Andrea raised her head and looked around. The room was featureless, but she noticed that a metal hook had been hammered into the opposite wall and a pulley was hanging from the ceiling, a white rope dangling from it. Pedro had been busy. She wondered what else he had in store for her. She hadn't the faintest idea what she was going to do to resolve this worrying predicament.

But it did occur to her that after a week or two Pedro might tire of his new toy. The effort of looking after her, of feeding her and making sure she was freed so she could use the bathroom, would become irksome and he would decide he'd made a mistake. Then hopefully he would free her, though she doubted he would take her back to Isabella. Alternatively, she might find an opportunity to escape. If she could somehow get some clothes and money, she could ring Charles Hawksworth and try to explain to him what had happened. Hopefully he would trust her word and intercede with Isabella, but as there was absolutely nothing she could do at the moment to help herself, she decided she had better go along with Pedro's plans and do whatever she was told.

'Did you sleep well?'

To Andrea's utter astonishment the door of what she thought of as her cell had opened and Carrie, the plump slave from the castle, had walked in. She was wearing a pair of denim shorts and a tight boob-tube, her midriff bare, the chubby waist and thighs exposed.

'What the hell are you doing here?' Andrea said, so surprised she tried to sit up, forgetting she was tied to the bed.

'Pedro made me an offer I couldn't refuse.' She grinned. 'And I was getting fed up with all the dike stuff anyway.'

'But I thought you liked it.'

'A girl can change her mind. Anyway, he said he had a job for me. He's really got into this master thing. And he's loaded. This house is vast. He could get at least another two or three girls in this basement.

And he's got a place in the country too. He's going to make me his major-domo. Like Dallas.'

Carrie sat on the edge of the bed. The metal cuffs around Andrea's ankles were clipped to a short chain attached to the wooden leg. Carrie unlocked the cuff on the left ankle with a small key, then pulled it over to the right and used the snap-lock to join the two cuffs together, before releasing the right from the bed.

'He forced me to come here,' Andrea said.

'Yeah, he told me. Told me I'm to be extra careful to make sure you don't get tricky. You're going to be in bondage until you learn to behave.' She followed the same procedure she had used on Andrea's ankles when it came to the cuffs on her wrists. 'All right, get up and have a shower. I'll be back with your breakfast later.' She walked out and locked the door behind her. Andrea was desperate to pee and struggled into the shower room, the ankle cuffs making it impossible for her to take more than the tiniest of steps.

The fact that Pedro had somehow managed to proposition Carrie and bring her to the house was depressing. It meant he was taking this seriously, and with Carrie to look after her it was unlikely he would tire of his new game. She showered as best she could with her hands and feet bound and managed to partly towel herself dry. The basement room was warm and sunlight streamed through the glass blocks in the narrow windows.

Carrie returned twice during the day with meals. She left some books and magazines for Andrea to read, a refinement she had not enjoyed at the castle. On the other hand, Carrie made no attempt to free her from her bonds, afraid no doubt, that she might attempt to overpower her and make a bid for freedom.

It was about an hour after the sun had set and she

had put the stark overhead light on that she'd heard footsteps approaching her door again. This time it was Pedro. He was wearing a white shirt and a pair of slacks, and carrying a nylon holdall. There was a riding crop tucked under his right arm.

'Good evening,' he said. 'Did you enjoy my little surprise?'

'Yes, master,' Andrea said quietly. She had decided during the course of the day that there was no point in antagonising him. The best course of action was to try to please and appease him.

'So, have you decided to co-operate?' he asked.

'Yes, master.'

'Good... stand up.'

Andrea had been sitting on the bed when he came in. She immediately got to her feet.

'Will you put these on for me?' From the bag he extracted a black satin waspie and a pair of black stockings with lacy welts.

He threw the whip and the bag on the bed, then took the key to the cuffs from a pocket and knelt at her feet, unclipping the metal hoops.

'I think we'll leave your hands for the time being,' he said. He took a roll of bandage from the bag. 'Hold them out in front of you.'

Puzzled, Andrea obeyed. Pedro pushed the metal cuffs up her arms as far as they would go, so they were clear of her wrists, then began winding the bandage around them. When they were padded he tied the bandages off and eased the cuffs back down.

'We don't want the metal chaffing your pretty little wrists, now do we? Raise them above your head.'

Andrea obeyed. It was a terrific relief to at last be able to draw her legs apart and she flexed the muscles of her thighs as Pedro wrapped the corset around her body and did up the hooks and eyes that fastened it at the back, clenching it tightly around her waist. The top of the garment fitted just under her breasts while the hem cut across her belly, the long ruched black satin suspenders hanging down her thighs.

'You can manage the stockings,' he said.

Andrea sat and pulled them on, using both hands, smoothing the silky material over her legs. She clipped them into the suspenders. The tops of the stockings were high, and she had to adjust the suspenders to hold them taut.

Pedro's eyes were fixed on her erotic beauty. She could see a bulge distending the front of his trousers. 'May I, master?' she said. Pedro didn't know the rules. He didn't know that slaves were not supposed to address their masters unless ordered to. But Andrea suddenly had an overwhelming yearning to feel his powerful erection. All day she'd had little else to do but think of it, and the bondage they'd left her in had created all sorts of desires.

'Of course, slave,' he smirked, understanding her request and unzipping his fly. The tip of his cock sprang free, the glans smooth and purple.

Andrea dropped to her knees and sucked on it delicately, running her tongue around the ridge at the base of the glans. She used her fingers to pull the rest of it out of his trousers, then thrust forward so it was buried in her mouth and her lips were brushing the metal zip from which it emerged.

'Hey, you started without me!' The door had opened and a tall man stood watching. He had a large round stomach, a sturdy neck, and arms and legs that looked like tree trunks. His face was squat, like a boxer who'd been in too many fights, and he was bald.

'Miguel, welcome,' Pedro greeted his friend, his root still embedded deep in Andrea's mouth.

Miguel said something in Spanish.

'Remember,' Pedro interrupted, 'we agreed to speak in English with the girl.'

'Sorry, I forgot. I love the outfit.' He repeated himself in the correct tongue.

'Oh, I've a lot more for her to wear.'

'I bet you have,' Miguel laughed. 'Now, I need a shower - I've come straight from work.' He walked into the shower room and turned it on. 'Is she good at that?' he called out.

'Excellent. But I think she'll be even better if I warm her up first.'

'Warm her up?'

'You'll see.' Pedro pulled his cock from Andrea's mouth. 'Stand up,' he ordered abruptly. 'Over here.' He pointed to a spot immediately under the pulley. Andrea obeyed quietly - she had little choice.

Pedro slipped the white rope from the pulley and tied it to the metal cuffs. He then pulled, drawing Andrea's arms into the air until they were stretched above her head. He tied the rope off on one of the wall bars.

After spending the night with her arms tied in this position, having them stretched up again renewed all the cramps and aches that had built up in her shoulders and arm muscles. She groaned softly.

Miguel emerged from the shower room, his body glistening with drops of water. Though he had a large stomach the rest of his body rippled with firm muscle. Like Pedro he was hairy, though much more so, his chest and legs covered with a thick mat, and some growing on his back. There was a tight tangle of curls around his uncircumcised cock, which was still flaccid. 'She looks good,' he said.

Eagerly, Pedro pulled his clothes off too. His cock was already erect. Miguel came up to Andrea and cupped her breasts, squeezing so his fingers sank into the pliant flesh.

'Stand aside,' Pedro said. He picked up the riding crop from the bed.

'You're going to whip her?' Miguel looked astonished.

Pedro nodded. 'That's what they like. Isn't it Andrea?'

'Yes, master.' There was no point denying it. Andrea's buttocks had already begun to tingle in anticipation. She felt the familiar rhythmic pulse in her vagina.

Pedro smiled his satisfaction, and then slashed the whip across Andrea's backside. A line of searing pain burnt into her. The second stroke was lower and harder, aimed at the underside of her bum just above her thigh. The milky flesh quivered invitingly. She gasped, but it was not a gasp of pain. The extraordinary pleasure the pain never failed to produce had already begun to course through her veins.

'Did you hear that?' Pedro said. 'I told you they all love it.'

Thwack! *Thwack*! He aimed carefully so that each stroke created a new angry line across the pert curves of her bottom.

Andrea wriggled her buttocks from side to side, trying to fan air across them, the four weals radiating heat.

'Feel it,' Pedro urged huskily.

With a look of astonishment, Miguel put his hand on her bottom. 'So... so hot,' he breathed.

'Go on, feel between her legs,' Pedro encouraged.

Miguel looked a little uncertain. 'Listen, Pedro,' he said. 'With her tied it makes me feel like we're... you know. And I don't want to do that.'

'She may be tied up, my friend, but that doesn't mean it's against her will. This is what she wants. There were five other girls up there, all like her. This is what turns them all on. Tell him, Andrea.'

The cool touch of Miguel's hand made Andrea gasp. The whipping had made her sexual nerves churn. It wasn't only the physical sensations; standing before the two men with her arms bound above her head and her body cinched into a satin corset, her bottom reddened and radiating heat, excited her intensely. It had been three days since she'd last had Pedro's penis inside her, and she was rapidly beginning to crave more of the same. 'Please feel me, master,' she pleaded.

Miguel tentatively put his hands on the welts of her stockings. Andrea moved her legs apart slightly as he moved higher. A second later she felt fingers nudging into her sex. He turned his hand, so his palm was cupping her vagina. 'She's so wet,' he whispered. 'I wouldn't have believed it, unless I'd felt it for myself. Just the whipping does that?'

'And the bondage,' Pedro confirmed. 'The two go together.'

'But I thought she was reluctant to come here.'

'She's reluctant all right. Some nonsense about another master back in England. But that doesn't mean she doesn't get herself in a state. She was the same at the castle.'

'And all the girls there are like this?'

'All of them. Carrie tells me there are girls who get thrown out of *The System* - that's what they call it -

but who are still desperate to have a master. She thinks she can find me one or two. That would be special, wouldn't it? I could entertain all my friends, just like my aunt does up at the castle.'

'Well, what are we going to do now?' Miguel asked earnestly.

'Stand in front of her, my friend,' Pedro invited.

Miguel faced Andrea. His cock was now fully erect.

'Lift her legs.'

Miguel's large hands caught Andrea under the thighs and lifted them so they were poised on either side of his hips, and his cock nudged into her sex.

'Mmm... I can feel how hot she is.'

Now Andrea understood why Pedro had used the bandage for padding; hanging thus the cuffs would have cut into her wrists.

Miguel bucked his hips, lifted Andrea slightly higher, and thrust his cock up into her. Andrea moaned and her head fell back. Her vagina clenched around him. She crossed her ankles in the small of his back and pressed herself down, wanting to get him deeper.

'My turn now, I think,' Pedro said pensively, almost to himself. He went to the bag, took out a small glass bottle, poured a colourless oil into his palm, and lovingly coated it over his erection. Andrea watched dreamily, and immediately knew his intentions.

He moved behind her, squeezed his hands between her and Miguel to cup her breasts, and kissed her shoulder. His slimy cock nudged deep into the cleft of her buttocks and she pushed back against it, almost without thinking. The red weals stung as they rubbed against his groin, but that only increased her arousal.

'Just relax,' Pedro coaxed. His glans nosed against her rear entrance.

Relax was the last thing Andrea could do. Her whole body was alive. Miguel's cock had already affected her so much, the way her sex was stretched around it, creating such a panoply of sensations that she was already on the brink of coming. This new penetration would, she knew, plunge her into orgasm.

Pedro pressed forward. The little ring of muscles resisted then almost immediately gave way, the slick of oil aiding his entrance in one long smooth thrust.

Andrea cried out, the paradox of pleasure and discomfort just about indescribable. Pleasure overcame her, sweeping through her body like a wave. And then her orgasm broke. She curled her hands around the rope above the leather cuffs and levered herself up, then sank down again, every muscle in her body rigid, every sinew on tenterhooks.

Pedro ground forward, pushing even deeper inside her. She could feel him sliding against Miguel's erection, both of them hard and pulsing.

They ploughed in and out of her. Andrea was whimpering continuously. She felt Miguel changing his rhythm. His fingers dug into her thighs, just above her stocking tops, and he screwed his eyes shut and bit her shoulder to stifle his groan as he came in her clutching depths.

At that moment Pedro toppled over the edge too. He shunted forward one more time, his hands clasping more urgently around her breasts and his penis spasming violently as he came deep in her bottom.

Miguel heaved a deep breath and eased away as Andrea's stockinged feet slipped to the floor. He slumped onto the bed, weary but satiated. Pedro withdrew too. He went to the wall and released the rope. Andrea's arms flopped like a dead weight. The cramp in her shoulders was so intense it made her cry out. She rubbed her arms as best she could with her hands still bound together.

'On your knees,' Pedro commanded. Andrea knelt in front of him. He hooked one hand around the back of her neck and fed his softening cock into her mouth. It was sticky with his spunk. She sucked him in, running her tongue along his shaft. Her juices had mingled with his, and she felt him growing already. In seconds he was fully erect again. She concentrated on him, pulling back until her lips were wrapped snugly around the distinct ridge at the base of his glans.

'You do like pleasing your master, don't you,' he stated triumphantly.

Chapter 9

'Very pretty. Bring her in, Carrie.'

Carrie nudged Andrea in the back and she walked forward. Pedro was lying on his antique four poster bed, his body wrapped in a dark blue silk robe. He put down the book he was reading and examined Andrea from head to foot.

Carrie had dressed her in a sheer nylon catsuit. The nylon was the same denier that was used to make stockings, so her breasts and her mons were veiled but not hidden by the material. The outfit was crotchless, the area between her legs completely exposed. Naturally, she was in bondage, her wrists bound behind her back with leather cuffs. There was no need to hobble her legs; the height of the shoes effectively making it impossible for her to take more than the most diminutive steps.

Carrie brought her to a halt in front of the bed.

Apparently she already had her instructions. The posts were thick and elaborately carved. She reached up to the frame that ran along the length of the bed between the top of the posts and pulled down a rope that was tied to it. She moved Andrea around so she was facing the bed and her knees were against the mattress, then looped the rope into the central link of the leather cuffs around her wrists and pulled until Andrea's arms were hauled up behind her back and she was forced to bend forward over the bed. Quickly Carrie tied the rope securely to the cuffs, making it impossible for Andrea to straighten up. There were two lengths of white nylon rope lying on the bed. Taking one of them she wound it around Andrea's left ankle, pulling her leg towards the post at the foot of the bed, then tying the rope to it. She looped the other rope around Andrea's right ankle and jerked on it hard, forcing her to spread her legs wide apart, then tied it to the bottom of the post at the head of the bed.

Pedro rolled towards Andrea and stared at her sex. He raised a hand and stroked her labia. With her legs splayed so far apart the mouth of her vagina was open and she could feel his fingers tentatively exploring the already sticky flesh.

'You're very good at this,' Pedro said, looking up at Carrie.

'I had it done to me enough times. There aren't many positions I haven't been tied into.'

'I think you deserve a reward, don't you?' He rolled back into the middle of the bed, unknotted the belt of his robe and pulled it apart. His cock had already started to unfurl.

'Now that's what I call a reward,' Carrie said, grinning.

'She can watch for a change,' Pedro sneered.

Carrie was wearing a dark green sheath dress. But as she unzipped it and pulled it off her shoulders Andrea was sure she had come prepared for this eventuality. Under the dress she was wearing a tight scarlet lace basque with long satin suspenders, flesh-coloured stockings and tiny panties that barely covered her mons.

'Pull the bra down under your tits,' he said.

'Just looking at you is making me wet.' She folded the bra cups down. From the back the panties were no more than a thin ribbon of material that cut up between the fat cheeks of her buttocks. As she leant forward, cupping Pedro's cock in her hand and feeding it eagerly into her mouth, Andrea could see that the gusset of the panties had virtually disappeared between the folds of her sex.

'Let's give her a little treat,' he said to Carrie, nodding towards Andrea.

Apparently Carrie knew what this meant. She opened the drawer of the bedside chest, rummaged inside, then extracted an odd looking tube made from black rubber. One end of the tube ended in a bulbous oval ball the size of a small lemon, with a tiny valve at its neck. The other end branched into two, each fitted with a flaccid black rubber bag.

Carrie took a small jar of cream from the drawer then moved behind Andrea. She undid the jar and dipped her fingers into it, scooping out a large gob of oily cream and smearing it all around Andrea's anus. Then she took one of the soft rubber bags and stuffed it unceremoniously into the little puckered hole, until it had completely disappeared and only the black tubing stuck out. Quickly she forced the second bag into Andrea's sex. She needed no lubrication here, however; Andrea's own juices copious enough to make the penetration effortless. The oval ball at the other end of the tube hung down between her legs.

Carrie took hold of the ball and turned the valve. She then began pumping the ball.

Andrea felt the strangest of sensations. The two rubber bags were being inflated inside her. In seconds the rubber was pushing out against her inner flesh, the two bags separated only by the thin membranes of her body. She felt herself being stretched, the rubber pressing outwards, moulding itself to the dimensions of both passages.

She looked up at Pedro. His eyes were focussed on her.

'Does that feel good?'

Andrea could only close her eyes and gasp.

'Come here, now,' Pedro said to Carrie. She knelt on the bed at his side, took his cock and fed it into her mouth, making sucking noises as her head bobbed up and down, her body moving in synch with her mouth. Pedro moaned loudly.

'Now why don't you sit on it?' Pedro suggested. He knew the physical torments it was possible to inflict upon a slave; the whippings, bondage, nipple clips and dildos that could cause pain and discomfort, but he had shown no knowledge of the mental tortures that were far harder to endure. Until now, that is. The sight of Carrie, pulling the thin ribbon of the panties to one side and straddling his hips, her sex poised above his glistening erection, reminded Andrea of the sort of torture she had endured with Charles Hawksworth. Despite the delicious sensations that pervaded her sex, to be made to watch another slave being allowed to pleasure her master while she was patently ignored, was the worse form of neglect and the hardest to bear. She could see him looking at her, and was sure he was looking for signs of her distress.

Andrea tried to tell herself that he was not her master and never would be, and that it didn't matter what he did or with whom. But whether because of her own instincts or the training she'd been given since first meeting Charles, it was impossible not to wish it was her and not Carrie that was being allowed the privilege of his cock.

'Get on with it now,' Pedro ordered.

'Yes, master,' Carrie intoned. Slowly she sank down on him.

Andrea felt her own muscles clench around the two rubber bags.

'Now fuck me.'

Immediately Carrie began riding him, her thighs and buttocks driving her up and down. But Pedro was not looking at her. He was staring straight at Andrea.

Carrie increased her rhythm. Andrea could tell she was coming, and then Carrie tossed her head back and let out a raucous cry.

'Now it's my turn,' Pedro said, his eyes still turned towards Andrea. 'Use your hands.'

It took a moment or two before Carrie recovered and managed to climb off, and then she obediently started to masturbate him. He moaned and thrust his hips up, arching his buttocks off the bed, and as Carrie's hand pumped his glans swelled and a parabolic arc of spunk shot up into the air. It splashed down on his chest and belly, pearly white in his black hair. There was a second, less powerful eruption, then Carrie squeezed his cock gently, and more spunk oozed out over her fingers. Eagerly she sucked her fingers into her mouth, licking them clean. Then she leant lower and licked up every last drop. She fed his glans into her mouth after that and tongued that clean too.

'Now let's play with her,' Pedro said, nodding towards Andrea.

'Mmm... sounds like a good,' Carrie purred. 'You know she's not allowed to come, don't you? None of the slaves are.'

'What do you mean?'

'The masters don't allow the slaves to come. That's a rule. And if they come without permission they are punished.'

'But how can they resist?'

'They are supposed to be trained. She's been to a woman in France. Very expensive.'

'Like a finishing school,' Pedro said pensively.

'Of course,' Carrie went on, 'if the provocation is too much, then they get the punishment.'

'I can see I have a lot to learn,' Pedro conceded, with a glint of hunger in his eyes. 'Why did she not tell me this?'

'Isn't it obvious? She doesn't think you're her real master. She's not going to make life more difficult for herself.'

Pedro smiled. 'So Andrea, you have been enjoying yourself at my expense, eh? Well, that's going to stop right now. You are not allowed to come until or unless I give you permission. Is that understood?'

Andrea damned Carrie under her breath. 'Yes, master,' she said, knowing it was asking the impossible. After everything she'd seen, after the feelings that rubber balls had created, and the way the tight bondage was affecting her, she was once again throbbing with sexual need. She would never be able to hold back her orgasm. She knew why Carrie had told him, however. If she was unable to hold herself back it would no doubt be Carrie who would be given the task of administering her punishment. The girl was obviously thoroughly enjoying her new role, and the more she was given to do the more she would relish it.

Carrie rolled onto her back and squirmed until her head was immediately under Andrea's belly and her hair was brushing against her legs. She lifted her arms, wrapping them around Andrea's bottom so she could lever her head between her thighs. Immediately Andrea felt her tongue pressing into the slit of her labia. Though the rubber ball in her vagina filled her completely the tubing that extended from it was thin and had not forced her labia apart, as a dildo would do. Consequently, Carrie's tongue had to burrow into the sticky wet flesh as it searched for Andrea's clitoris.

'Ohhh...' Andrea exclaimed as she felt Carrie's tongue butt up against her swollen clit. It moved across it gently, creating a huge kick of sensation that made Andrea moan anew.

'She likes that,' Pedro said enthusiastically. He sat up, propping himself against the pillows, watching intently. Andrea raised her head to look at him. He had taken his cock in his hand and was wanking lazily, the shaft still wet with Carrie's juices. It was already beginning to engorge again. 'Must be hard for her to resist all that,' he said to nobody in particular.

Fingers probed Andrea, following the two tubes up into her and poking at the inflated rubber balls, thrusting them deeper. The slippery rubber seemed to reform itself, nudging into new areas, moulding itself to the inner contours of her body. But it was the way the balls rubbed against each other as Carrie's fingers prodded at them that gave Andrea the greatest thrill, the interaction of the warm slick rubber crammed so tightly into both passages of her body creating a whole new series of sensations.

The trouble was that nothing was isolated. The way Carrie's fingers were making the balls move inside her connected directly to the feelings her clit was generating as the girl artfully wriggled her tongue against it. And the tight bonds on her ankles and wrists somehow amplified all these feelings, as if being tied so tightly made it impossible for them to dissipate. Separately she might have been able to resist the power of these different provocations, but together they were irresistible.

Though her neck muscles protested she raised her head to look at Pedro. 'Please...' she begged.

He was clearly delighted with this. He laughed, his eyes sparkling with excitement. 'Now she begs me. She has never done this before. Of course you are right. Slaves should not be allowed to come. They should have to suffer.'

His hand was still working at his cock, which was fully erect now, his smooth glans projecting from the circle of his fist.

Carrie's tongue worked on Andrea's clit relentlessly.

'Please...' Andrea repeated. Desperately trying to stave off the inevitable, she raised her head and tried to push her body up vertically and twist away from Carrie's eager mouth. Unfortunately, not only did she not manage to accomplish either objective, but this manoeuvre produced a spasm of pain in her ankles, shoulders and arms, pain that inevitably translated itself into a pleasure that suffused and intensified everything she was already experiencing.

But it was not just an attempt to save herself from Carrie's punishment that made her try to fight back her orgasm. Though she knew perfectly well that

Pedro was not her master, her commitment to obedience was absolute. The aching frustration, the agony of being tormented like this - as Isabella had tormented her - was all part of being a slave. And the effort of trying to control herself, of trying to be a perfect slave, only added to her frustration. The more she struggled to stop herself from coming, the more she strove to be the perfect slave, the more excited that made her. But she knew she could not hang on for much longer, and it was Pedro who proved to be the final straw.

He got to his knees on the bed and crawled to Carrie's side, so his erection was poised mere inches from Andrea's mouth. 'Suck it,' he said.

Andrea turned her head and pressed her lips around his glans. The feel of that hot hard erection, tasting of male seed and female juices, the way it pulsed as she slid her mouth onto it, was too much to bear. Her clit spasmed and despite all her efforts, her cunt and anus clenched around the slippery rubber balls, making them recoil sharply, all sensations combining to break the last thread of control and send her pitching into orgasm. Her whole body shook, her mouth closing around his cock as she tried to suck in air. The orgasm was so intense, when it was over and she opened her eyes again she wasn't at all sure where she was. The bed was empty. Then she felt an odd feeling between her legs. Her sex and her anus felt as if they were shrinking. In the fog of bewilderment her orgasm had created it took a while to work out that Carrie had opened the valve and the rubber balls were deflating. The sensation made her moan, little trills of pleasure reviving what she had felt moments before.

Carrie jerked on the tube and the flaccid rubber balls were pulled clear. Immediately Andrea felt another sensation. Pedro was standing behind her. His hands gripped her hips and his erection slotted into her sex. He plunged into her. She gasped. He filled her completely, his glans forging deep.

Pedro pulled her back against him as he thrust forward. He pumped in and out of her a couple of times. Then he withdrew from her vagina altogether and without pause, impaled her bottom. There was no resistance. The rubber ball had left her open and accessible; the oil Carrie had used still providing extra lubrication. Pedro's cock thrust right into the depths of her, making her gasp again. She knew he was coming. She knew him well enough to recognise the signs; his cock throbbing insistently, his breath short and rasping in his throat. He pounded into her bottom three or four times then, as smoothly as before, lanced his cock back into her vagina.

This treatment was driving Andrea wild. In seconds she was on the brink of an orgasm again. Looking down between her legs she could see Pedro's phallus, glistening with her juices, sawing up between her hairless labia, the whole area of her sex neatly framed by the tight nylon catsuit. She could see something else too. Carrie had moved behind Pedro and was pressing her body against his, squirming her breasts and the red basque against him. Her hand delved down between his legs and Andrea saw her fingers cupping his balls.

She felt the effect this had on him, too. As if his cock had suddenly been shot with a bolt of electricity, it quivered inside her, swelling and hardening further, both of which she would have believed impossible. This in turn set her off. But as she felt herself come, as the first signs of orgasm lanced through her nerves, Pedro pulled out again. This time he paused, waiting at the little puckered mouth of her bottom, deliberately teasing himself, as well as her.

'Shall I?'

'Please... please...' she begged, as fervently as she had before.

Andrea saw Carrie squeeze his scrotum again and at that moment he plunged his cock deep into her most intimate passage, as deep as it had ever been. There was a momentary stab of pain, then the inevitable surge of pleasure as her orgasm took her over once again, the fact that it had been delayed mid-spate making it even more powerful.

Pedro sawed into her, ignoring the way her body was trembling. He gripped her hips more tightly, thrust forward one last time, then waited. She felt his spunk pumping up his shaft, but then it stopped, as though dammed. For what seemed an eternity Andrea held her breath, her eyes and mouth wide, and then with Carrie's hand milking his balls, he erupted, the dam breached and the viscous fluid anointing Andrea, propelling her over the edge into the abyss of a violent climax.

Eventually he sat heavily on the edge of the bed, his exhaustion obvious. 'Cut her down,' he said.

Carrie obeyed immediately. She released the rope that held Andrea's arms and Andrea collapsed forward onto the mattress, too numbed to move. Carrie knelt and untied her ankles.

'So, what did you say I must do now?' Pedro asked.

'She disobeyed you, master,' Carrie pointed out.

'And disobedience means punishment?'

'Exactly.' Carrie looked exceedingly pleased with herself.

'Do you have anything appropriate in mind?'

'Isabella always used to say that the punishment

should fit the crime.'

'She did? Well, I couldn't agree more.'

'Then why don't you leave it to me, master?' Carrie offered, her tone dripping with eagerness as she eyed Andrea with a mixture of lust and spite.

'Now, why don't I do just that?'

Andrea had spent the next day in her cell. She imagined that Pedro still thought she might try to escape, which was why he did not give her any domestic duties around the house during the day, as Isabella had done. From what she had seen of it on her way to his bedroom, though the house was large it could be seen from the road, and with the curtains and blinds open in daylight she should be able to attract attention. If Pedro intended to set up an establishment here he was going to have to make sure his slaves were well trained.

Andrea had now been with Pedro for three days. She remembered Dallas telling her that Isabella was going to be away, so she doubted that her disappearance from the castle would yet have been reported to Charles Hawksworth. But it was only a matter of time. And that was what depressed her most. If Pedro had been part of *The System*, if he'd bid for her at the auction and she'd been delivered to this house, she would have been only too pleased to be his slave and serve him as unquestioningly as she had Charles. But he wasn't and hadn't.

Carrie had delivered her breakfast, and returned later with lunch, but it was not until the sun had set and no more light filtered through the glass blocks in the narrow windows that she finally unlocked the door of the basement cell with something else clearly on the agenda. She was wearing a pair of tight black trousers and a plain white blouse, knotted at the waist. Andrea could see she was not wearing a bra.

'Stand up,' she said, dropping a small bag on the bed.

Andrea obeyed, not wishing to make things worse for herself.

'Over here,' she ordered, indicating a spot against the wall bars.

'Where's Pedro?' Andrea asked tentatively.

'He'll be here, don't worry.'

Carrie took a pair of leather cuffs from the bag. She buckled them around Andrea's wrists then again pulled her arms up over her head, using a short length of rope to tie the cuffs to one of the bars.

She ran a hand down Andrea's body, flicking her fingernails against Andrea's vulnerable nipples. She cupped both of Andrea's breasts, squeezing the flesh, then leant forward and kissed her, pressing their lips together. Despite disliking the girl, Andrea felt a surge of arousal. As Carrie's tongue wormed into Andrea's mouth she ran a hand down between her legs, a finger nudging against Andrea's clit. She rubbed it subtly.

'This is something I thought of myself,' Carrie said, pulling away. There was a note of pride in her voice. She extracted a leather strap and buckled it around Andrea's waist. Hanging from the back of the strap was a thick piece of black rubber. Carrie went back to the bag and pulled out a double dildo, shaped like an extended thumb and first finger, though a great deal bigger. She knelt at Andrea's feet.

'Open your legs,' she said. 'If you don't I'll have to go and get a leg-spreader.'

Andrea saw no choice but to obey, and as she did Carrie pushed the dildo up between them. Her earlier assault had left Andrea wet and Carrie rubbed the smaller of the two up and down the crease of her sex until it was coated with her juices. Then she reversed it and unceremoniously pressed both shafts deep into her body. Andrea moaned as both her passages were invaded.

Carrie reached down between her legs and pulled the rubber strap up against the flat base of the dildo, holding it in place. The rubber strap was split into two thinner strips at this point which, when Carrie had looped them up along the creases of Andrea's pelvis and tied them to the waist belt, left the top of her labia completely exposed.

'I'm going to get Pedro now,' Carrie told her. 'Then we'll begin. I'm going to turn both vibrators on and give you a little whipping. Of course, you won't be allowed to come. How long do you think you can hold out this time?' She laughed.

Carrie picked up the bag, then dropped it again. 'Silly me,' she said. 'I forgot the most important bit.' She reached into the bag and pulled out a thin chain. It was T-shaped, with a clip at each end. Andrea had seen the clips before. They were metal and spring-loaded, their serrated jaws designed to bite into the soft flesh of a nipple.

Carrie ambled back to her victim. Holding the short bar of the T out in front of her she opened one clip threateningly. 'I always used to hate these,' she mused.

She positioned the clip over Andrea's nipple and allowed the metal jaws to close. Andrea winced as the tiny teeth bit into her. The stab of pain was followed by an equally affecting wave of pleasure, which was routed directly to her sex. Carrie noted her tremble. 'You love them, don't you?'

Andrea said nothing. She waited as the second clip

was positioned. The trouble with not being given anything to do during the day was that she had so much time to think. And naturally enough, she had dwelt on everything that had happened to her the previous night, and what was due to happen to her tonight. That meant her whole body was sensitised, her nerves wired and waiting. Which was why, she told herself, she reacted so strongly to Carrie's sadistic attentions.

The second clip bit into her nipple. She shuddered, then gasped, as a second wave of pleasure joined the first. But Carrie hadn't finished yet. There was a third clip at the end of the chain, which now hung between Andrea's breasts, nestled in her deep cleavage. It was much bigger than the other two.

Carrie knelt in front of Andrea. She opened the clip with her right hand and moved her left to Andrea's sex lips, framed by the black rubber straps. She parted the pliant hairless flesh until she found the pink promontory of her clitoris.

'No...!' Andrea cried, suddenly realising what she planned to do.

'Oh yes.'

The metal jaws sunk into the flesh on either side of her clit, pinching the button of nerves between them. But this time there was no pain; at least there was no pain that was not striated with the most intense pleasure. For a moment Andrea actually thought she was going to come. Carrie pulled the chain upward, and Andrea's clit reacted violently.

'Please... you can't leave me here like this,' she pleaded. The shock of pleasure had left her panting for breath. The trouble was that the chain that ran down her body was so tight that every time her chest rose, the chain was pulled up and dug into her clit more deeply, causing excoriating pleasure and pain.

'See you soon,' Carrie said, smiling. She stroked Andrea's cheek. A film of perspiration had already formed on her forehead and Carrie wiped it away. 'Just imagine what it will feel like when the vibrators are turned on.' She turned and left Andrea alone, not even bothering to lock the door.

Andrea tried desperately to control her breathing so her breasts would not rise and fall so dramatically. But it was a vicious circle. The harder the clip bit into her clitoris the more she needed to suck in air, and the more her chest rose. The more her chest rose the harder the jerk on the chain attached to the clip and the more deeply it bit into her. And that was not all. The clips on her nipples were pulled tighter too, creating yet another source of that unique blend of pain and pleasure that affected her so deeply.

Slowly, very slowly, she managed to get herself back under control.

Somewhere in the distance she thought she heard a dull thud. She tried to convince herself she no longer cared about Carrie and Pedro, and what they would do to her, but as she saw and heard the door slowly creaking open she closed her eyes fearfully and held her breath.

'My, you *do* look a mess.'

Andrea froze in disbelief. She knew that voice, and it wasn't Pedro or Carrie. Slowly she opened her eyes, and there in the doorway, stood Dallas Fox. 'I - I don't understand,' Andrea blurted. Perspiration had run into her eyes and she shook her head to try and clear her vision.

'I've come to rescue you,' Dallas said calmly, gliding into the room. 'Not particularly comfortable accommodation,' she said scornfully.

'Dallas,' Andrea warned, 'Pedro's going to be here soon.'

'No, he's not,' Dallas said definitely. She moved to Andrea and examined the chain. 'Ingenious. Who did this to you? Carrie?'

Andrea nodded.

'Mmm... I might try this myself. It looks as though you've been enjoying yourself.' She ran a hand under the vertical chain, tugging it slightly. Andrea moaned, the clips immediately creating new waves of conflicting sensations. 'Prepare yourself,' she warned, gripping one of the nipple clips and opening it. After being trapped for so long the nerves responded with an acute spasm of pain. A second followed as the other clip was removed. Dallas stooped and carefully removed the third clip from between Andrea's legs, causing the bound girl to whimper pitifully, then unhooked her wrists from the metal ring.

Andrea found herself shaking uncontrollably. She managed to untie the two ends of the rubber strap between her legs from the belt around her waist and tentatively allow it to drop, holding the double dildo in place with her free hand before allowing the inert lengths to slip gently from her body.

Dallas watched intently. 'Well, they thought of everything, didn't they?' she said, as she watched the two dildos, glistening with Andrea's juices, emerge. 'No wonder you were in such a state.'

'H-how did you find me?' Andrea asked weakly. She was feeling totally confused, and finding it difficult for her to grasp what Dallas' arrival meant. Would she be taken back to the castle? Did Isabella know what had happened? Questions crowded into her head.

'I was coming to your room that night, remember?'

Dallas explained. 'Just as I started down the walkway I saw them carrying you out. I got into a car and followed them. Lucky I did. I don't suppose Isabella would ever believe you'd been abducted by her precious Pedro.'

Andrea went uncertainly into the shower room and picked up a towel, using it to dry off her perspiring body. 'Why did you wait so long before coming for me?' she asked over her shoulder.

'I wanted to make sure Pedro was acting on his own. If his big friend was in residence or he had other guests, I would have needed reinforcements. So I watched the house for a couple of days until I was sure. Come on now, we'd better go before Pedro wakes up.'

'Wakes up?'

Dallas winked and smiled conspiratorially. 'Did they give you any clothes?' she asked.

'Um, no...' Andrea's mind was still in a spin. 'Only, um, lingerie, and they take that away every night.'

'Don't worry - we'll find you something.

'Wh-what happens to me now?' Andrea asked, not really sure that she wanted to know the answer.

'I take you back to the castle and explain to Isabella what happened. She'll no doubt want to have a few words with her nephew. He was enjoying your company all the time he was at the castle, right?'

Andrea nodded, and then added hastily, 'But I didn't seduce him, I promise you.'

'I know. Don't worry.'

Dallas led the way out of the room and into the corridor. They walked carefully up the basement steps into the hall by the front door. Carrie was lying on the floor. She was gagged, blindfolded and hog-tied; her wrists bound behind her back with rope and her ankles pulled up to join them.

'I see you've woken up,' Dallas said, kneeling at the girl's side.

Carrie struggled, trying to say something through the gag. All that came out was some mumbled grunts. Dallas tore open the trussed girl's blouse. Andrea realised she was still holding the T-shaped chain. Dallas grasped Carrie's breasts and despite her desperate struggles when she saw what Dallas intended, pinched the clips to her nipples. She then held up the third clip. 'I'd like to put this on too, but there's no time.' So she dropped the chain on the tiled floor.

'Aren't you going to take her back too?' Andrea asked.

'No. She's made her choice. Isabella will inform her master what's happened and what she did. Her name will be wiped out of *The System*.'

'They were planning to get other girls here, not just me.'

'We'll see what Isabella has to say about that. By the time she's spoken to his father I don't think Pedro's going to be in a position to do anything much.'

Dallas stepped over Carrie's neatly packaged body. 'Come on, we can borrow some of her clothes for you.'

They walked upstairs. The door to Pedro's bedroom was open and Andrea glanced inside. Pedro was lying on the bed in his silk robe, apparently fast asleep. There was a strong smell of chloroform in the room.

Dallas followed Andrea's gaze. 'I followed him to a bar a couple of hours ago. He thinks he's so attractive to women it was not difficult to convince him I was smitten and get him to invite me back here. I suggested we came straight up here...' she laughed. 'And then I dealt with Carrie.'

They opened all the doors along the landing and found Carrie's room, her clothes strewn untidily over the furniture and floor. Andrea picked up a yellow blouse and skirt and hurriedly put them on, even though they were too big.

'Come on,' Dallas said.

As they walked back past Pedro's bedroom he groaned. He was trying to sit up. The effort was too much and he fell back on the bed, holding his head and mumbling something in Spanish.

'He's going to have a terrible headache in the morning,' Dallas said, and began to laugh.

Chapter 10

Dallas unbuttoned the jacket of her suit. As she was not wearing a blouse there was nothing to cover her lacy black bra, her breasts straining against it, the bra cups cut so low they barely contained the soft flesh. She reached behind her back and unzipped her tight skirt, wriggling her hips until it fell to the floor and she could step out of it. She was wearing black lace panties and her glossy gunmetal-grey stockings were hold ups, the narrow bands of elastic that formed their welts clinging to the flesh at the very top of her thighs.

Andrea looked at her body. It was undoubtedly one of the most beautiful female bodies she had ever seen; sleek, smooth and supple with not an ounce of fat, her skin radiating health. Her belly was flat and her buttocks round and pert.

They had driven back to the castle while Andrea related everything that had happened with Pedro, both at the castle and at his house. She explained that she was afraid Isabella would think her to blame for him finding out about the slaves, and that he threatened to lie if she didn't keep quiet. She was still worried that Isabella would blame her for what had happened, but Dallas assured her she would explain that it was definitely not Andrea's fault and that she had been kidnapped.

With Isabella not due to return until the next day Dallas had taken Andrea up to her bedroom. Like all the bedrooms in the castle it was large and luxurious, with a thick cream carpet and oatmeal walls. There was a large en suite bathroom too, where Andrea took a long and leisurely bath while Dallas went downstairs to check on the other slaves. She was now lying on the large double bed, the sheet underneath her made from silk.

The American unhooked her bra, letting her breasts spill from the lacy black cups. Her nipples were knotted and erect.

'We shouldn't be doing this,' Andrea said, without conviction.

'Do you want me to tie you up? Would that salve your conscience?'

Andrea shook her head. Despite the excesses endured at the hands of Pedro and Carrie, the sight and fragrance of Dallas induced a surreptitious pang of desire within her. Of course, she knew she should not be there; if Isabella found out her major-domo was using the slaves without permission they would both be punished. But for once, she didn't care.

Dallas skimmed the tiny black panties down her long legs, kicked off her shoes, pulled her stockings off, and sidled sexily into the bathroom. Andrea heard the shower running.

Hesitantly, she stretched her legs apart, running a hand down between them. She inserted a finger into her sex and probed her clit. Closing her eyes dreamily, she quivered delicately and swooned.

'Would it be better if I did that?' Dallas asked huskily. She was standing in the bathroom doorway with a towel in one hand, her body shimmering with droplets of water. The lights in the bedroom had been dimmed, so her slender body was silhouetted against the bright light from the bathroom. She reached inside the door and flicked the bathroom light off, the silhouette turning to a voluptuous shadow. Walking over to the bed she towelled her body perfunctorily.

'Are you sore?' she asked gently.

'A-a little,' Andrea stammered, suddenly feeling like a timid child.

Dallas opened a drawer of the bedside cabinet and took out a small tube. 'This will help,' she said. She knelt on the bed beside Andrea and squeezed some of the cream onto her palm. 'I use it sometimes on the slaves if Isabella has been a little enthusiastic. It stings at first, but then it feels wonderful.'

Very carefully, Dallas rubbed her palm against Andrea's nipple. As she said, the cream tingled quite severely as it was massaged into the puckered bud. But the heat dissipated and as Dallas spread the cream out, encompassing Andrea's voluptuous breast, it seemed to soften the edges of her tortured nerves. Dallas stopped momentarily to apply cream to her other palm, and then began massaging both breasts. Soon the therapeutic purpose of the massage was forgotten and Dallas was kneading Andrea for entirely sensual reasons, moving the mouth-watering orbs of flesh in circles, the cream that was not absorbed by the skin leaving a silky sheen. She moved both hands to Andrea's nearest breast, moulding it firmly, then leant down and sucked it gently into her mouth, flicking with her tongue.

The soreness disappeared. Andrea wanted this so much. And, for once, being free, being able to move her arms and legs, felt good. She wanted to be able to please Dallas, not only as a way of thanking her for what she had done, but because she felt a real aching desire to touch and caress her. She allowed Dallas to move over to her left breast and perform the same gorgeously sensual procedure there, but then, as her hands rolled her flesh between them, she pushed up off the bed. It was such a novelty to be able to use her hands that she saw they were trembling as she took Dallas' face between them and kissed her. As her tongue delved tentatively the American's moved against it, hot and wet, the two dancing together, vying for possession of each other's mouth.

Dallas sank back. Andrea rolled on top of her without breaking the kiss, the sensation as their breasts moulded against each other making her shudder. The American opened her legs and Andrea instantly slipped a thigh between it, pushing up so it was pressed tightly into the humid apex. The mouth of her vagina was leaking wetness that was soon smeared over her skin. Dallas hooked an arm around Andrea's back and, without breaking the sensual kiss, rolled them both over until she was on top. It was her turn to grind against Andrea and push her thigh up between Andrea's legs.

'You feel so soft,' she whispered, finally pulling her lips away from Andrea. 'I'm really turned on.'

'Let me do it to you,' Andrea panted.

Dallas smiled. 'What a good idea.' She rolled off Andrea then came up to her knees. Swinging one leg over her shoulder she straddled Andrea's head, facing her feet, her sex open and poised above Andrea's mouth.

Andrea stared up at her. She could see the neat, puckered fistula of her anus and, below it, the mouth of her vagina. It was glazed with the sap of her arousal.

Before Dallas could lower herself Andrea hooked her arms around her thighs and levered her head up, planting her mouth firmly on her sex. She twisted her face from side to side, lapping at the juices that flowed over her tongue.

'Yes...' Dallas breathed. 'Just like that...'

Within a few seconds Andrea felt Dallas tense, the sinews of her thighs tightening against her face. She reached out blindly and brushed Dallas' breasts, then pinched her nipples, sinking her fingernails into them.

'I'm coming...' Dallas breathed, her back straight. As Andrea's hands fell away Dallas gripped her own breasts. Her orgasm broke over the tip of Andrea's artful tongue, her body rigid.

For a long while they remained locked together, Dallas enjoying the aftermath of her climax. Eventually she rolled off Andrea and they lay side by side on the bed.

'Roll over, on your back,' Dallas said.

Andrea did as she was told, and Dallas took a pair of leather cuffs from the bedside chest, pulled Andrea's arms behind her back, and buckled the cuffs tightly around her wrists. 'No one must know what we've just done,' she whispered. 'It's just between the two of us. Next time we're together it'll be different. You understand that, don't you?'

The new tension in Andrea's shoulders and arms from the sudden bondage created all sorts of very familiar sensations.

'It turns you on, doesn't it?' Dallas said.

'Yes... it does,' Andrea admitted.

'Yes, what?' Dallas said sternly, her attitude completely changed, her usual dominance reasserting itself.

'Yes, Ms Fox.'

'That's better. Now, roll over and move your legs apart.' Dallas walked across the room and came back with a metal leg spreader and a rubber paddle. She dropped the leg spreader between Andrea's ankles, and buckled the cuffs at either end of the metal bar to them. She was smiling a knowing smile. 'I was a slave once,' she said. 'Did you know that?'

Andrea shook her head.

'Oh yes. To an American, in Boston. He was very strict. He made me wear corsets so tight I could hardly breathe. And shoes that tipped my feet as if I was on points. It was agony - but I loved it. I know what you need Andrea. I needed it once myself.'

Dallas raised the paddle and slapped it down on Andrea's thighs. It was a completely different sensation from being whipped. With the whip the pain was sharp and linear. With this rubber paddle the whole of her thighs seemed to sting. The second stroke was aimed at her breasts, making the milky flesh quiver. She smacked again, both strokes leaving red blotches on the white skin.

Andrea's body was alive again, writhing on the bed, her nerves wired by this treatment. Being free to express her gratitude to Dallas, as exciting as that had been, was a completely different experience from what she was feeling now. It had been exciting, but it did not compare to the indescribable edge, the intensity, that she'd felt as soon as Dallas strapped the leather cuffs around her wrists. It was perfectly true; she did need the bondage and the submission.

She wondered if Dallas felt the same. She could see the lust that glinted in her eyes. It had not been there as she'd smoothed the soothing unguent on her nipples.

Dallas dropped the paddle on the bed and opened another drawer in the bedside cabinet. She pulled out a long double dildo. 'Now, let's see if we can get you to give me some real pleasure.'

Dallas climbed back on the bed. Without ceremony she fed one end of the dildo deep into Andrea's vagina. She held it firmly in one hand while she straddled Andrea's hips, then fed it into her own sex.

'Now fuck me, slave,' she said between clenched teeth.

The shiny black PVC was tight, and so was her bondage. Dallas had decided it would be best for her to explain what had happened as soon as Isabella returned home, and wanted Andrea on hand appropriately dressed in an outfit which emphasised her dedication to her role as a slave.

The garment she wore was a full-length boned corset, laced with scarlet red laces down the front. It had a quarter-cup platform bra that lifted Andrea's breasts, but left them completely exposed, and suspenders that had been clipped into shiny black stockings of the same stretchy material. Her nipples had been given special treatment; they were rouged with a dark red blusher then snapped into little hinged gold rings that fitted tightly around their base, squeezing the flesh out prominently.

She was not wearing panties. Two of the slaves had arrived that morning and taken her into the bathroom, spending a long time shaving and oiling her sex until it was absolutely smooth, with a sheen like the finest silk.

As for her bondage, Dallas had produced long leather gloves, but they had two distinctive features. At the top of each one was a thick leather strap that wrapped around Andrea's shoulder and under her arm. Each glove also had a flange of leather on the inner surface that was perforated with metal eyelets. As soon as Andrea wriggled her arms into them Dallas buckled the top strap tightly over her shoulder, then pulled her arms behind her back and threaded lace through the eyelets, slowly but inextricably knitting her arms together. By the time she reached the top, Andrea's arms were pressed so closely together and protesting under the unbearable strain.

A pair of black patent leather ankle boots, also with red leather laces, with a heel so high the soles of Andrea's feet were almost vertical, completed the outfit.

Isabella was expected at eleven. At ten-thirty Dallas had taken Andrea into the large sitting room to the right of the front door. And there she stood, with Dallas sitting on one of the sofas, waiting for her fate to be decided.

Dallas heard the car first and jumped up. 'Come on,' she said.

As Andrea struggled to walk across the room, tottering so much in the high heels she thought she might fall, Dallas opened the front door. The black limousine came to a halt, the tyres crunching on the gravel.

The sun had almost reached its zenith and it was a

hot day. The heat that rushed in from outside was in marked contrast to the cool interior. As Andrea positioned herself just behind the door, she felt perspiration breaking out on her forehead.

Dallas, wearing her businesslike black suit, walked outside and opened the passenger door before the chauffeur could do so. Despite the heat Andrea felt a cold chill seize her body. It was not Isabella who got out of the car - it was Pedro.

'How nice to see you again,' Dallas gushed.

'Is it?' The chauffeur had walked quickly but majestically around to the other side of the car and opened the rear door there. Isabella had stepped out. 'Let's go inside,' she added, her voice cold and strident.

They marched inside the castle. As Pedro looked Andrea up and down he grinned. Isabella led the way into the sitting room. 'Bring her in here,' she barked.

Dallas took Andrea by the arm and led her in.

'Right, so tell me exactly what's been going on,' Isabella demanded. She was wearing a cream silk dress, very sheer flesh-coloured stockings, and cream high heels. She sat in a large wing chair, crossing her legs, giving a glimpse of stocking top before she pulled her skirt down over them.

Dallas began uncertainly. 'It - it started when Pedro came to visit...'

'No, no, no,' Isabella interrupted. 'I know all about that. I know all about her. What interests me, Dallas, is you.'

'Me?' Dallas said.

'Yes, you. Didn't I specifically tell you that you were not allowed to have any of the slaves without my permission.'

'I...'

'Answer me!'

'Y-yes, you did - but I don't see what that's got to do...'

'And despite that instruction,' Isabella continued relentlessly, 'did you take her...' she pointed at Andrea '...and other girls to the punishment rooms and sometimes even to your bedroom?'

Dallas lowered her gaze meekly and began to blush. 'I... only after you'd told me I could,' she said, floundering.

'Did I ever give you permission to have her?' She nodded at Andrea again.

'No, but...'

'No. Never. But how many times did you in fact amuse yourself with this one?'

Dallas did not reply, but Andrea sensed she was no longer going to tough it out.

Isabella turned the screw a little more. 'Answer me.'

'Th-three or four times,' she mumbled without looking up.

'Exactly.'

How on earth did she find out? Andrea wondered. But almost before she'd asked herself the question she knew the answer. Carrie. Carrie had obviously heard them leaving her room together. Or perhaps just guessed. Whichever it was she had told Pedro and Pedro had told his aunt. Things were going from bad to worse.

'All right, I'll deal with you later,' Isabella said sternly. 'Now bring the girl forward.' Dallas took hold of Andrea's arm and led her to Isabella's chair. 'Now it's your turn,' the woman said to Andrea. 'Are you going to tell me what has been going on between you and my nephew?'

'He - he kidnapped me,' she blurted. She had been

expecting Dallas to do all the talking and had not prepared her own speech.

Pedro laughed derisively. 'Yes, of course I did,' he said sarcastically.

'Did you have sex with him while he was staying here?' Isabella asked, her eyebrows knotted in a frown. 'Despite my specific instructions not to.'

Andrea knew denial would be pointless. 'Yes, mistress,' she admitted humbly. 'Yes, I did.'

'How often?'

'Over four nights.'

'I see. And did you tell him about what goes on here - about the slaves?'

'No, mistress, I did not. He knew all about that already.'

'And he came to your room and demanded you have sex with him?'

'Yes, mistress,' Andrea confirmed quickly, a little hope dawning, 'that's exactly what he did.'

'And I suppose I threatened you by saying I'd go to my aunt and tell her you were the one who seduced me?' Pedro sneered.

'Yes, that is what you did,' Andrea said, turning to challenge him. If looks could kill he would have withered on the spot.

But he merely laughed scornfully again. 'I told you,' he said, turning to his aunt.

'And this apparent kidnapping,' Isabella continued. 'That is your excuse for running away and hiding yourself in the boot of his car? Is that correct?'

'He came back with a friend,' Andrea gabbled, sensing the situation turning against her again. 'They tied me up. I had no choice.'

'I came back to get some books I had forgotten, like I told you, aunt,' Pedro said convincingly.

'That's not true,' Dallas protested. 'I saw them, Marchessa. I saw them carrying her to his car. She was all trussed up. I followed them to his house. She was his prisoner.'

'You're not going to believe anything she says, are you aunt?' he scoffed. 'She's lied to you already. She's just trying to get back at me for telling you the truth about her.'

'If you wish to continue working for me, Dallas, I suggest you say no more,' Isabella admonished curtly. 'Pedro came to my hotel last night. He was in a terrible state. He said he wanted to tell me everything that had happened.

'This girl,' she indicated Andrea with a dismissive wave of a hand, 'has obviously become infatuated with him. I can understand why; he's an attractive young man. But that does not excuse what she's done. Apparently she arrived at his house and begged him to be her master. She told him she would do anything he wished. Naturally, he told her she should leave at once, that he wanted no part of it, but she refused. He had to throw her out physically. That shows a strength of character few men would possess in the face of such provocation. It was admirable.

'Obviously I have had to take Pedro into my confidence about what goes on here. He has faced that with equanimity too. When he is a little older I've told him he can come here as my guest and take full advantage of all our facilities.'

'I'm not sure I really want to do that, aunt,' he said obsequiously. 'You know my feelings. I think I'm a one woman man.'

Andrea felt sickened as she watched him feign embarrassment.

'That is your choice, Pedro, of course. And I respect

it. Meantime,' she turned to Andrea, 'take her back to her room. She specifically disobeyed me. There is only one course of action I can take. I warned her. I will phone her master and arrange for her to be sent straight back to London.' Isabella got to her feet. 'After that is done,' she smiled that cruel smile of hers and turned towards Dallas, 'if you wish to continue here, we shall have to find a rather unique punishment for you. I think I have something in mind - I'll let the slaves punish you. It will give them an opportunity to get their own back.' She chuckled. 'Come on, Pedro, I need a drink before lunch. I hope you'll stay the night.'

'I'd be delighted to, aunt,' he said, smiling like a schoolboy who'd just received a good report.

'Be quiet, don't say a word.'

It was dark. The corridor light was turned off so no light spilled into the room as the door was opened. Andrea started awake. She could only see the vaguest silhouette looming over her. As an extra punishment Isabella had ordered that she could sleep in the tight PVC corset, the stockings and the boots, as well as being tied spread-eagled to the bed.

'Who is it?' she asked timidly.

'Don't worry, Andrea. It's me.' It was a man's voice. For a moment Andrea could not place it. Then her heart stood still. She recognised the voice. It was her master, Charles Hawksworth. But how could it be? He was in London with a huge business empire to run. How could he have come to Madrid in the middle of the night just to see her? Was she dreaming?

'Master,' she said, so taken aback she could think of nothing else to say.

'Yes, it's me. Dallas Fox telephoned me. She told

me what happened. She told me everything. I came right away.'

'But... what time is it?'

'Four in the morning.'

Andrea felt tears prickling at her eyes. She could not believe he had done this for her. 'I - I didn't do it, master,' she sobbed, her emotions suddenly getting the better of her. 'I promise I didn't.'

'I know, I know,' he said reassuringly. 'That's why I came. You're very special to me, Andrea, you know that, don't you?' He stroked her forehead. Even in the dark she could see his steel-blue eyes looking straight into hers, those hypnotic eyes that simply beguiled her. She certainly did know that now. 'Thank you, master.'

'I'll talk to Isabella in the morning. But I had to see you first. I'm going to turn on the light now. Close your eyes.'

After a few moments she opened them again. Charles Hawksworth was standing by the door, looking immaculate, as usual. 'I approve,' he said, examining her carefully. 'I see she's had you shaved.' He was staring at her sex.

'Will I be sent home, master?' she asked.

He shrugged. 'It's Isabella's decision. That is the way *The System* works. But I think I have a plan that may change her mind.'

'I didn't do it,' she repeated.

'I know.' He sat on the edge of the bed, still looking at her body. He ran his hands over her breasts, making her shudder. It was as though his hands were wired to an electric current. 'What does this feel like?' A hand glided over the slippery PVC and down between her legs. Very gently he parted her labia. 'Being shaved, I mean. Do you like it?'

'If you do, master, then I do.' Slaves were not supposed to express their preferences.

Charles smiled. 'Marie-Claire trained you well.' His finger arched inward, parting the soft tissue. She felt it nose into the mouth of her vagina. 'So soft,' he said.

The finger probed. The surprise of his arrival had not given Andrea's body time to react to his presence, and she was dry, the finger having to prod against the inner flesh before it could press forward. But suddenly she moistened, and his finger slid deep. 'So responsive,' he added.

He bent forward and kissed her nipple, the rings that had been closed over them keeping them erect. She felt his teeth fastening around the stiff bud as he pressed two more fingers into her sex. She gasped loudly, the mental relief and the idea that her master would actually come all this way just for her, creating just as much arousal as the physical sensations. Her sex clenched around his fingers.

'There are no prohibitions tonight,' he whispered. 'You must come for me. I want to see that.'

'Oh, master.' Andrea was trembling. She pulled against the bonds, arching off the bed and trying to push herself down on his fingers. She ground her hips from side to side on his hand.

Charles moved his mouth to her other nipple, biting it just as hard and making Andrea moan again. Then he leant forward and kissed her lightly on the lips, his eyes staring directly into hers.

Her nipples ached where his teeth had been, but it was a glorious sensation. She was already coming. She fought to keep her eyes open, wanting him to see her orgasm through them, but as ecstasy overwhelmed her they clamped shut.

'Quite lovely,' Charles whispered. His hand pulled

away from her sex, making her sigh.

'Thank you, master,' she whispered, her mouth dry.

'Take this now.'

Such was her delirium she had not noticed Charles take his cock from his trousers. It was fully erect and throbbing. He knelt on the edge of the bed and thrust it towards her face. She welcomed it dreamily between her lips. The feeling of having him in her mouth almost made her come again. But she managed to control herself, focussing on his pleasure. She sank on his erection until it was nudging the back of her throat. Then she started to smooth her lips back up his shaft.

'No,' he stopped her sharply, his fingers clamping in her hair. 'Like you were.'

She immediately sank back onto his rigidity. After a few minutes she felt him swell even more, and then he groaned and her mouth filled with his viscous offering. She swallowed avidly, and a second eruption bathed her throat.

Wake up, master, wake up.'

Pedro was sleeping in one of the guestrooms, but not the one he had used on his earlier visit. It was mid-morning and the sun was trying to slant in through the narrow gap in the heavy curtains.

'What is it? What time is it?' he blurted, sitting up abruptly and staring around the room.

Andrea knelt on the bed. She was naked, apart from black hold up stockings and a pair of black high heels. They had left the rings on her nipples, the metal pinching them into permanent erection. 'It's me, Andrea,' she said softly.

'What the hell are you doing here?' he demanded aggressively, rubbing his eyes. 'I thought they'd got you under lock and key.'

'They had. I escaped. They arranged a van to take me to the airport first thing. Dallas handcuffed me to the seat in the back, but I think one of the locks is faulty.' Andrea held up her left wrist. A pair of cuffs dangled from it, one hanging open. She snapped the open loop closed, but it fell open again. 'When the van stopped at the main road I slipped out. Isabella and Dallas have gone into Madrid, so we're all alone.'

'Why didn't you just run away while you had the chance?'

'Because of you.'

'What do you mean?' He was looking at her hungrily, his eyes riveted to her breasts and ringed nipples.

'Pedro, don't you see?' she purred sexily. 'Those days with you were the most exciting in my life. You must have seen that for yourself, how you made me come so exquisitely. I want to go back with you. I want you to be my master. You said Carrie was looking for renegade girls - girls who'd been thrown out of *The System*. Well, I'm one of them now. I want to be with you, master. Please take me home with you.'

Pedro sat up. He rubbed his eyes again as if to make sure this was not a dream. 'Really?' he said.

'Oh, please. Please let me come with you. I've dreamt about you every night. All those things you did to me. It was Dallas. You know that. She didn't give me a chance. She used that chloroform on me, too.'

'So why did you tell my aunt it was my fault?' he demanded suspiciously.

'Because I hoped she wouldn't send me away and I'd be able to escape and come back to you,' she said without faltering. 'That would have been the easiest way. But she was determined. If it hadn't been for these...' she held up the handcuffs '...I'd be on my way to London by now, and I've no idea what they'd do to me when I got there. They said they'd release me, but I think they'd punish me first. I might not have been able to get back to you for months.'

'All right, calm down,' he said. 'Let me think.' He got out of bed, naked, and Andrea saw her chance. With sensual agility she slipped to her knees and fed his flaccid penis into her mouth. Pedro was clearly taken aback, but couldn't suppress a moan as her lips tightened around him and her tongue ran over his glans. His cock began to stiffen rapidly.

'Please, master,' she cooed, pulling away, massaging his cock and staring up at him with what she hoped was an adoring gaze. 'Don't I please you? I thought you wanted me, too.'

'Um - what time are they expected back?'

'We haven't got much time.'

He thought quickly, her teasingly gentle hand getting him flustered. 'All right,' he decided.

'Really?' Andrea jumped to her feet and hugged him, kissing him on the lips and grinding against him. His cock, trapped between them, pulsed against her belly.

Twenty minutes later Pedro was dressed. 'All right,' he said to Andrea, 'let's go.'

'Please, master, I know I shouldn't ask, but would you do one other thing for me?'

He looked at her irritably, and then at his watch.

'Tie me up,' she went on.

'What on earth for?'

'Because you are my master now. And bondage makes me so excited. Tie me up and let me spend the journey on the floor of your car. I'd be so excited when we got home I'd be melting. I'd do anything you want. Anything, master.' She saw a glint of excitement in Pedro's eyes. 'The chest of drawers, master. This is one of the special guestrooms. That's why they didn't let you sleep here before. These rooms have all the equipment the guests might want to use on the slaves.'

Pedro opened the drawers, one by one. He pulled out a long coil of white nylon rope.

'Okay,' he said, 'turn around and put your hands behind your back.'

'Yes, master,' Andrea said solemnly.

She felt him knot one end of the rope to her wrists then wound the rest of it up around her arms to just above the elbow. Despite the situation, she felt the usual tingle of excitement emanating from her sex.

Pedro looped the rope around her body under her breasts, then around her back again. This time he pulled it over the top of her breasts so they were pinched between it. He did this several times, pulling the loops tighter each time, and then tied it off. 'Is that what you wanted?' he said.

'Yes, master. I really feel like your slave now.'

'And this is what I want,' he added, going back to the chest and extracting another coil of the same rope. This time he knotted it tightly around her waist and pulled it between her legs, cutting deeply into her sex. He jerked the rope into the cleft of her buttocks and tied it tightly to the rope at the waist.

'Pretty,' he said. 'Turn around.'

The slightest movement of her legs made the rope chaff against her clit and her labia. She moaned softly.

'That will keep you interested until we get home. Just imagine the welcome Carrie will have for you.' A large bulge distended the front of his trousers. Binding her so tightly had excited him. 'Perhaps I should have a little taste now,' he said.

'There's no time, master,' she objected hastily. 'We've got to get away before they come back.' She nodded at the clock on the bedside table.

'You really want this, don't you?' he gloated.

'Oh yes, master, I really do.' She looked straight into his eyes and tried to look as sincere as possible.

Pedro opened the front door. 'Come on, I can't wait to get you home,' he said, taking her by the arm and leading her out into the warm sunlight to where his car was parked on the drive. He opened a rear door and pushed Andrea inside. 'Get down on the floor,' he ordered, watched her obey, his eyes glinting with lust, and then slammed the door shut.

He got behind the wheel and started the engine. The large wooden gates were open. But as he began to drive towards them they swung smoothly shut, and a tall figure with steel-blue eyes appeared in the middle of the drive. Pedro hit the brakes and the figure advanced towards the car, just as the front door of the castle opened again and Isabella and Dallas appeared.

The man with steel-blue eyes opened the passenger door and began pulling Andrea out.

'Well, Pedro,' Isabella said, 'how are you going to explain this?'

Pedro jumped out of the car. 'You bitch!' he hissed at Andrea. 'You tricked me!'

'Tricked you?' Isabella mused. 'How could she do that? According to your story, Pedro, you were not at all interested in her even when she begged you to be her master.'

'I wasn't - I'm not,' he stammered. 'I was just doing this to prove to you exactly what she's like.'

'Despite the fact you thought I wasn't here. It's not going to work, Pedro. No more lies. Tell me the truth. It was you who threatened Andrea when you were staying here, right? And you who kidnapped her.'

Pedro's shoulders sank. 'All right,' he mumbled, 'yes.'

'Good. Then we've got that straight.' She turned to address Charles Hawksworth, who was holding Andrea affectionately. 'Charles, I've a lot to thank you for. As much as I adore Andrea, I think by way of making things up to her I should let her go back to London with you.'

'Oh, mistress, thank you. Can I really do that?' she said, looking eagerly at Charles.

'You belong to Isabella until the six months is up,' he pointed out. 'So it's up to her what happens to you.'

'I'm sorry I doubted you, Andrea,' Isabella said, and then turned to Dallas. 'And you, Dallas.' She took her hand. 'I'm sure I can find a way to make it up to you.'

'I'm sure you can,' Dallas said.

'So why don't you take Andrea inside, Charles, and get those ropes off. Do it somewhere nice and private. I'm sure it will be most enjoyable.'

Charles smiled. He looked at Andrea's trussed body. 'Most enjoyable,' he agreed.